Menace in Red Chaps

**Center Point
Large Print**

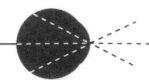

**This Large Print Book carries the
Seal of Approval of N.A.V.H.**

Menace in Red Chaps

Eli Colter

CENTER POINT PUBLISHING
THORNDIKE, MAINE

This Center Point Large Print edition
is published in the year 2010 by arrangement with
Golden West Literary Agency.

The text of this Large Print edition is unabridged.
In other aspects, this book may vary
from the original edition.
Printed in the United States of America
on permanent paper.
Set in 16-point Times New Roman type.

ISBN: 978-1-60285-711-7

Library of Congress Cataloging-in-Publication Data

Colter, Eli.
  Menace in red chaps / Eli Colter. -- Large print ed.
      p. cm.
  ISBN 978-1-60285-711-7 (library binding : alk. paper)
  1. Large type books. I. Title.
  PS3505.O368M46 2010
  813'.52--dc22
                                        2009045408

CONTENTS

CHAPTER . . . . PAGE

I. Bad Man of the Secos 7

II. Rendezvous 15

III. A Fool for Blue 28

IV. The Devious Heart 50

V. Lobo Pass 75

VI. The Man from Chicago 88

VII. Who was the Other Man? 103

VIII. Puzzle for Lispy Louie 118

IX. Kurt Rides Again 142

X. The Web Tightens 161

XI. Lon Tells a Story 181

XII. Dead Men Tell too Little 192

XIII. The Valley of Death 212

XIV. Redemption 242

CHAPTER I
BAD MAN OF THE SECOS

THERE are only two ways by which a man can be redeemed; by atonement, or by death. In either case, the price paid for the redemption must be the life of the redeemed; life given in willing endeavour to the retraction of wrong doing, and to the building of a future so valiant and so beyond reproach that the discarded past is cast forever into the shadow; or life laid down in heroic sacrifice that the better may survive and clouded issues be cleared, or merely that the slate may be wiped clean of a worthless existence. The decree is absolute. Always the accomplishing of redemption takes one of these two courses. Sometimes it takes both.

In the hot, early-morning sun, in the town of Seco Springs, at the edge of the Seco Mountain foothills, five ranch hands gathered before the bar of the Idle Hour Saloon. They were all talking at once, in that tautness of voice that makes for a strained monotone. They sounded like a lot of angry bees buzzing. The tenseness of the air was such that a man could feel it; he would have needed a skin thicker than cowhide not to feel it.

The five ranch hands were pronouncing the

ultimatum that the only redemption possible for Kurt Quillan must be death.

Quillan had been going his own sweet way and killing as he pleased all over the Seco for better than a year. Had he bothered to keep count, there would have been some seven notches on the butts of the heavy calibre guns he carried; only Kurt never bothered. He had never bothered about much of anything. Whenever anyone was so indiscreet as to cross his path, he merely looked the foolhardy one in the eye and said, "Start shooting!"

Helpless as the victim knew his action to be, he usually reached for his weapon and died, gun in hand, bested by the phenomenal draw of Kurt Quillan. Up till now, Kurt's killings had been visited upon obscure drifters of questionable repute, nondescript characters whose sudden death was unlikely to precipitate any vengeful act of retaliation.

But, two days past, he had crossed the dead line that had in the last twelve months preserved his hide whole, the dead line of fear that his reputation for accurate aim and ruthless action had drawn around him, clearing other men from his vicinity, rendering him immune to pursuit or reprisal. Two days past, near Seco Trail and west of Circle G Ranch, on the open range that lay in the middle of the Seco country, he had killed Lem Strickland. Eight notches for the gun butts now. And wild excitement, fired by fierce indignation, had been sweeping the Seco range ever since.

This was the last straw. The Seco range was "on its ear" from one end to the other. Of all the lowdown, dirty, unspeakable acts! Why, Lem and his wife had raised the shooting fool: had taken him in on the L-Over-S Ranch when he was only a baby, had brought him up in place of the children they had never had, had loved him like their own. Lem had taught him to shoot. Lem had made him a present of the finest horse ever bred on the Seco range, a magnificent Arabian of shimmering brown. Lem and Mrs. Strickland had done everything for him they could have done for their own son. And Kurt had thanked them by shooting Lem down.

Within two hours after Lem had died speedily from the fatal bullet, half the men of the Seco were banded together and started looking for the slayer: they had raked the occupied territory, the open range between, and now had advanced into the mountains to the north of the open range, beating every clump of brush, every grove of trees, every gully and draw, trying to flush Kurt into the open as a hunter and his game dogs flush quarry from cover. And they hadn't found hide nor hair of him. Not a track. Not a camp fire ash. They hadn't yet looked in the right place. They would, eventually, but he wouldn't be there.

The five ranch hands in the Idle Hour, who sounded so much like angry bees buzzing, had

9

been riding with the posse, and had dropped down into Seco Springs for a few hours of rest and a cool drink or two. By noon, they expected to be on their way again toward the mountains to the north. Their intense absorption was consistently ignoring "Swabs," the bartender. He didn't care for that. He wanted also to be heard. He cleared his throat loudly, to attract the attention of the angry men across the bar. They all turned their heads to look at him in scowling inquiry.

Whatever Swabs had intended to say, the words were never spoken. Swabs opened his mouth to give them utterance, but it stayed open, and he merely gulped, his eyes widening, staring out into the hot dusty street before the saloon windows. The five men across the bar whirled to follow his startled gaze. Another ranch hand, astride a big white horse named Skater, had just ridden up to the hitching rack. He dismounted, dropped Skater's reins over a post, and came toward the swinging doors of the Idle Hour like that famous irresistible force looking for an immovable object; in fact, the expression of his face grimly dared any immovable object to get in his way.

"Well, ain't that something?" ejaculated one of the men before the bar. "Bill Stagg, this far from the Circle G! We been wondering why he wasn't with the posse. Can't say as I like his looks any too well."

Swabs nodded concurring opinion, and closed

his mouth. His still dilated eyes were fixed on Bill Stagg, as Stagg shoved through the swing doors and strode up to the bar, the sawdust purling from each of his footlifts in a small dry shower. If he had any reputation greater than that of being the best top hand the Circle G ever had known, it was that of being eminently able to discern what constituted his own business, and of attending to it with notable efficiency.

Stagg was a huge man, so huge that he loomed high above the bar as he paused before Swabs; his shoulders were broad, his chest thick, his arms were long and his big hands hard and powerful. He carried himself with a peculiarly graceful assurance that is often common in men who mind their own business so well. His black hair was frosted at the temples. There were a few wrinkles around his deep-set black eyes. The rest of his face was smooth and young, as if no emotion ever trod there to leave its tracks.

Swabs, and the five ranch hands staring at Stagg, were sharply conscious for the moment of one paramount thought: Bill Stagg was the man who had found Lem Strickland and carried him home to the L-Over-S to die, and nobody had seen Bill Stagg since. He rarely came to Seco Springs; the town of Arroyo, the only other town in the Seco country, was many miles nearer the Circle G. Bill was so seldom seen off the Circle G that a large proportion of the Seco men knew him only by sight or reputation, and some of them didn't know him at all. Nothing short of an event ever brought Stagg clear across the open range to Seco Springs. Nobody in the silent room tried to guess what part of the Seco's latest tragic event had brought him here now. They waited for him to speak. He did, to the bartender.

"Give me a whisky, straight, Swabs. About four fingers."

Swabs complied with alacrity. "Sure. Sure! Help yourself!" He shoved a glass and an opened bottle down the bar.

Stagg filled and drained the glass with enviable evidence of his capacity to take it raw, before he spoke again. He set the empty glass down upon the bar without making a sound, and swung his huge, graceful body about with the peculiar lightness of perfect muscular co-ordination, and stood sidewise to the bar, so that he faced both Swabs and the group of ranch hands.

His voice was deep, it rumbled like an organ pipe, but it held an even pitch, and it betrayed no more emotion than his features.

"Boys, I've issued a challenge to Kurt Quillan. Kurt isn't up north of the open range where the posse is hunting for him. I know where he is, and I've sent word that I dare him to meet me here this morning; that I'll be waiting for him, and that I'll drag him feet first from the Idle Hour two minutes after he enters it."

Since it is a natural reaction for one suddenly startled badly to draw a sharp breath, every one of the six men facing Stagg did it. Such a challenge was tantamount to a declaration to commit suicide, and that wasn't exactly their idea of an amusing pastime. Was Bill taking leave of his senses, or was he for the first time in his history on the Seco range overtly concerning himself with another's affairs?

Something in Stagg's black eyes, cold and glittering as flint in the sun, seemed to advance violent negation to both questions. He saw their glances flick toward his waist, and divined their thought, which was a decidedly elemental task. With their attention centred in that direction, they could scarcely have but one thought. Their eyes were on the belts around his waist, gun belts, crossed, shell loops about half filled, a holster on each belt.

Another unprecedented historical event for the Seco: Bill Stagg wearing two belts. Bill was a fair shot, highly accurate, not very fast. So far as any one ever knew he had never shot anything other than coyotes, rattlesnakes, digger squirrels, and such other annoying pests. One gun sufficed. One belt.

But now he wore two belts. Two holsters. Both holsters were empty.

"B'golly," said Swabs, staring at the empty holsters. "Kurt Quillan coming here! You mean that?"

Stagg deliberately filled another glass, emptied it with the same finesse, and replaced the empty glass again on the bar with the same noiseless motion. The smile that touched the corners of his square strong mouth might have been designated as firm, sinister, mocking, or sad. It was all in the way you saw it.

"Nobody ever caught me fooling yet, Swabs," he answered. "And when he shows up, you boys keep out of it. He'll have a clear path from where he is to the Idle Hour. He isn't going to run into the posse, or anybody else. If he should, he'll know how to keep out of their way. I'm going to tie Skater in the shade. I'll be back in a minute."

He wheeled and walked out of the saloon, leaving both awe and consternation behind him.

Swabs expended his breath in a gust. "I'll believe anything now. You boys want a drink on the house? Better take it while you can get it. And you better get out of here before Kurt shows up, if you want to avoid contracting lead poison."

"I'll take the drink on the house instead," said the same ranch hand who had spoken before. "If any man can take Kurt Quillan, it's Bill Stagg. And if there are going to be any fireworks coming off, I'd sort of like to see the show. It ought to be good. I'm staying. The rest of you fellows can light out if you feel like it."

"No takers," said the fifth man down the bar.

"I'm not hankering to stop any man's lead, but I'm fool enough not to want to miss this. If it don't prove worth a little ducking and dodging, I'm a red-eyed bronc that'll never be branded."

CHAPTER II

RENDEZVOUS

WITHIN a few moments Stagg had led Skater from the hitching rack around to the shade of the saloon building, and returned to join the five men before the bar, still drinking on the house. The cowboy who had no hankering to stop any man's lead looked at Stagg with a speculative glance.

"How soon are you expecting him, Bill?"

"Well, he's cached in that open triangle between the north line of the Crazy L, and the top of the L I east line. It's about fifty miles from here to there. The fellow who saw him there and came to tell me about it, left the Circle G about the same time I did. He went straight up there, and I had a damn sight farther to ride. He must have passed my message on to Kurt nearly two hours ago. Kurt ought to be here by noon. That Arabian's fast."

Now, the lay of the Seco range was this: The great stretch of open range lay squarely in the centre, running north and south. In the north it ended in the Seco Mountains. To the south it widened and spread all over hell's half acre. Both Seco Springs and Arroyo lay to the south of it. West of the open range were two ranches, the Crazy L and the L I, side by side, miles north of Seco Springs. To the east of the open range lay four ranches: the L-Over-S, south of the railroad which ran through Arroyo; the Cross Bar, east of Arroyo; the Circle G, north-west of Arroyo and north of the Cross Bar; and the Seven Up, east of the Circle G. Such was the Seco range.

It covered a lot of territory, but all the men of the country knew it like a book. The five men before the bar, and Swabs behind the bar, could see in their minds' eye the course Quillan would take due south across the Crazy L and the open range below it.

"What was he doing up there?" Swabs wanted to know.

"Playing tag with Lispy Louie, Swabs." Stagg never grinned; had it been a tendency of his, he would have grinned then at the look on the bartender's face.

"Lispy Louie" le Grande owned the Crazy L. It was a small ranch and he ran it all by himself, but he didn't make a very good job of it. His brand fitted his outfit. Everything about the Crazy L was slightly insane. Louie was small, dark, with oily skin that perpetually shone as if he had just greased it. His eyes were smoky brown and one of them was cocked. He was sly and shrewd, he looked crazy and wasn't, and he was no fit company for a self-respecting cowboy. Swabs sniffed, trying to vision Kurt Quillan coming within a hundred yards of Louie without scaring him out of his greasy skin.

"Well, what did this fellow come and tell you for when he saw Kurt up there?" Swabs was given to asking rash questions.

"Because he was scared right out of his pants, Swabs, and he had to tell somebody, and he knows I never step on worms. Anything else you want to know, Swabs? Don't be bashful, step right up and ask." Was that warning in Stagg's black eyes, or amusement?

Swabs thought it was to be taken at face value as an unusually amiable and talkative streak in Bill Stagg. He leaned on the bar, agog with eagerness.

"Yeah. Who was the fella that told you and went back to tell Kurt what you said?"

Stagg's black eyes bored into Swabs, and for an instant all the men thought he was going to refuse answer. His reply, when it finally came, was harshly curt. "Lispy Louie."

"But—but—" stammered the bartender, over his head entirely. "If he was scared out of his pants even at sight of Kurt, how could you get him to go right up and tell Kurt that—"

Stagg cut him short. "You'll let all your brains run right out of your mouth some day, Swabs. What time is it?"

Swabs subsided, and glanced at the rusty old alarm clock under the bar. "Quarter after ten, Bill. Why?"

"I was just wondering how long I'll have to wait. Noon's the deadline. He won't be later than that."

Stagg missed accurate calculation by just eighteen minutes. At eighteen minutes before twelve Kurt Quillan rode up in a furl of dust, leaped off that finest horse ever bred on the Seco, and stood for a moment motionless, gazing intently through the saloon windows.

The outlaw was a man one would turn to give a second look anywhere—tall, straight, lithe, young. His hair was chestnut-brown and it glowed like fire in the sun. His eyes were long and wide apart, a cold, clean blue. His heavy lashes and brows were black. His features looked as if they had been chiselled out of some sun-browned stone, and by a skilful and fastidious hand. At each corner of his full, curved mouth a deep dimple drove into the flesh when he smiled, boring into the high colour blending from his cheeks, and when he stopped smiling there was a white spot where each dimple had been, till the colour rushed back. The process of that smile held the eye, like it or not, and his big but perfectly set teeth made one think of pearled marble, if there is such a thing. They made one think of it anyway.

But he wasn't smiling now, as he halted there, gazing levelly at the seven men who stood watching him through the saloon windows. His eyes were blue fire. His features were the colour of the paper sacks you get at the store. They couldn't turn white. His skin was too dark, both by nature and from exposure to the elements. He walked slowly across the intervening space between the hitching rack and the swing doors, and from the way he walked one would have felt certain that no matter what he was walking on he wasn't making any noise.

His hands were hanging at his sides. He opened the swing doors by the simple process of stepping forward till his body pressed against them and walked through them. He might have been a tornado, instead of a cat-footed killer, considering the reaction he got. As if blown aside by a violent gale, the five men before the bar swept back to the wall. Swabs stood petrified behind the bar; Bill Stagg stood carelessly leaning upon it.

Quillan moved toward the bar like something propelled gently through the air. There was about him the manner of some pulsing incandescent force, ready to explode into devastating activity at the slightest provoking or rude touch. It couldn't be said that he halted before the bar. He simply reached that position and ceased to move. His full, curved mouth showed the big white teeth when he spoke, and though his words held the substance of violence, his voice caressed the air like a muted A string on a guitar.

"Who the hell is Bill Stagg, barswabber? Who is he, and where is he? Tell him I'm here, and that two minutes can be a long time."

Swabs couldn't answer. His eyes bulged from the pressure of fear behind them. His teeth were clenched till they ached. His tongue filled his mouth, dry as cotton. He hadn't even enough control over his optical muscles to swing his gaze to Bill Stagg, though he did make the effort.

Quillan's blue eyes began to lose their fire, to turn cold and clean of all emotion. They moved in an arc from Swabs to the five men drawn along the wall and from the men along the wall to Stagg, still leaning on the bar exactly as he had been, waiting in silence. As Quillan's gaze came to rest on the huge man with the frosted black hair, it stilled. There was no need for him to ask again who or where was Bill Stagg. The answer to that question was quite apparent.

"I've been waiting for you," said Stagg, and the timbre of his deep voice might have indicated laconic reply, or curiosity, or some indescribable degree of pity—which wouldn't seem according to the cards; pity for Kurt Quillan! "You made good time. That Arabian must do about a mile in a minute flat if you shove him. Step up and I'll buy you a drink."

If the incandescent force which was the essence

of Kurt Quillan had been quiescent before, it was hushed now. Of all the situations he had estimated that he might find when he should confront Bill Stagg in the Idle Hour, he had never even remotely visioned this. A man must judge by his own standards of conduct, and he knew the potential devastation that hung by a hair trigger within himself when he faced a man as softly as Bill Stagg was facing him. In that instant Kurt Quillan came as close to fear as he had ever come in his life.

The sensation was as unwelcome as it was uncomfortable. Some intangible aura about him seemed to quiver. The fire burned high in his still eyes, blurring the clean cold blue.

"If you want a drink, you'd better get it quick. It may be your last, and you haven't much time. I don't drink—with fools."

Without a lowered glance, without a designating syllable, he referred clearly to the empty holsters Stagg wore.

"Nice of you." Stagg turned his gaze upon the bartender without moving his head. "Make it two whiskies, Swabs. Kurt always drinks with an old friend."

Swabs felt himself shivering again, but he didn't even try to stop it now. He knew he couldn't. Every moment the explosion of that quivering force pent in the outlaw was hovering nearer its detonation. Then Swabs's brain managed to do a little work on its own initiative without any impulsion from him. An old friend. Was that really what Stagg had said? Goofy! Why, Quillan hadn't even known who Bill Stagg was! Swabs's brain kept right on working now, though he was trying hard to make it stop; the conclusions it was drawing were frightening, and he was badly enough frightened already.

He dared a covert glance at the taut-bodied ranch hands drawn along the wall, and found that his eyes would really move. He found, too, that they were stumbling over the same obvious consideration that had started his obstinate brain functioning.

Bill Stagg. Kurt Quillan. Strangers to each other. An old friend. An old friend? An old score, that was the word. Some ancient call to redress, reaching back through the years. And Kurt Quillan was ignorant of it. This was nitroglycerine, and Bill Stagg held the detonating cap.

Swabs filled two glasses with whisky, and his fingers shook till the bottle clinked against the glasses' rims, then he dropped the bottle, and snatched at the neck to keep it from turning over, and wiped the sweat from his upper lip with the back of his hand. Neither Stagg nor Quillan looked at him. They looked at each other. Huge man with frosted black hair, and tall, lithe man with chestnut hair: black eyes, hard and cold, and blue eyes, blurred by fire, waiting.

Stagg picked up the glasses, he raised himself from his leaning position, drew his huge body erect, and advanced till he was within two feet of the outlaw. He offered Quillan the full glass in his left hand. The pulsing force blazed to life.

With his wild lightning draw, Quillan cleared his right-hand gun of its holster, crashing the glass from Stagg's hand, spattering the whisky over both of them. Swabs swayed and closed his eyes, setting his sick nerves for the blast that must surely follow. But no report of gunfire assaulted the aching silence of the room.

Stagg's huge hand, quite as swift as the slashing weapon, spurting blood from several cuts the shattered whisky glass had made, clenched into a fist and swung upward in a vicious arc that ended on the right side of Quillan's chin. The crack of the blow sounded like the popping of a frozen stick.

The quivering force went out so quickly that it was almost as if some one had turned off a light that was uncomfortably hot. Kurt's gun dropped into the sawdust. Kurt toppled and went over onto his back beside the gun, out cold, his jaw broken.

A painfully released sigh breathed from the five men along the wall, like a faint breeze.

Stagg raised the glass in his right hand and drained it, exactly as he had drained it before. Not a drop of whisky had spilled. He set the empty glass back upon the bar without making a sound. He tilted his head and looked at Kurt Quillan. He moved as if there were no one in the room but himself and the senseless outlaw whose chestnut head lay in the sawdust. The presence of others being largely an acceptance of one's own awareness, there were right then no others in the room but Stagg and Quillan—to Stagg.

He bent over Kurt. He picked up the gun in the sawdust, and took the other from Kurt's belt. He thrust them both into the empty holsters on his own belts, which had been waiting for them.

With one almost effortless heave and swing of his long arms and big hard hands, he lifted Kurt's inert body to his shoulder. He got no farther.

The street outside fogged with dust boiling from sliding hoofs; a dozen horses came to a milling stop at the hitching rack. Men thudded to the ground, and came racing into the Idle Hour. The ranchers' posse, with Pete Gulick at its head.

Pete Gulick was the little fat Dutchman who owned the Circle G. He was German, but the Seco called him a little fat Dutchman. His face was round, his head was tow, and he had a round fat little belly. His language was a sort of polyglot of broken English, guttural idioms, German ejaculations and incongruous slang. But he wasn't a comical figure. In spite of his plump stature and excitable ways, there was always about him an indefinable dignity. No man was better liked on the Seco. He was observant of eye and quick of perception; he grasped the entire significance of the scene as he halted short, the posse crowding at his shoulders, and saw his own top hand standing there with the outlaw's limp body held firmly by his raised left arm.

"Vait a minute, Bill!" Gulick commanded. "Ve cut Kurt's trail, and ve followed him in. Ve got bizness mit dot son uf a gun."

Stagg's deep bass muted to a smooth consonance. "Sorry I can't oblige, boss. I'm taking care of Kurt Quillan personally. You can mark this down in your little book: Kurt's killing days are over. What I'm going to do with him is my own damned business, in case you don't know me well enough to realize it. And I'm warning every man on the Seco range to keep his hands off unless he wants to get hurt. You all back over here along the wall by the other boys. I can use one of these guns of Kurt's if I have to. I'd rather not."

Gulick lifted a plump hand and gestured his men toward the wall. "Vell, don't you heard vot he said? Get out of his vay, yet!"

They moved almost as quickly aside as the other men had moved when Quillan entered the room. Stagg bent a queer smile on the fat little Dutchman. "Thanks, boss. Don't let any of them get out of hand, because I'll take a shot at a man for the first time, if anybody tries to stop me. I won't miss. What time is it, Swabs?"

25

"Four—fourteen minutes off twelve. Why?"

"Not bad calculating." Stagg gripped Kurt's body a little more tightly, and bent to pick up the outlaw's blue beaver hat lying on the floor. "I said I'd drag him out of here feet first two minutes after he came in. Four it is. However, seeing that I have my hands full, and he's banged up a little, I'll just carry him out feet first."

He turned and walked toward the swing doors, Kurt's limp legs thrusting out before him, and against his broad back, as he moved into the band of sunlight streaming through the windows, Kurt's chestnut hair glinted like fire, and three little flecks of sawdust fell from it, burning yellow for an instant in the hot sunlight as they drifted to the floor. The swing doors closed with a slight rasp.

Swabs slumped against the bar, and the colour began to return to his face. All along the wall the posse men started to galvanize into action. Before they had advanced three feet the little Dutchman barked at them.

"Cut dot out! Don't you heard vot he told you? All you boys stay right vere you are, yet. Bill Stagg knows vot he's doing, and you let him alone. You don't tink he pulled dot chust to be doing some monkey bizness, do you? *Nein!* Not Bill Stagg. I never did tink Bill Stagg comes to der Seco range chust to make vun more goot cowhand for de Circle Gee. Now I know it. And you punks stay put right vere you are or I raise hell mit you!"

No one answered him, verbally, that is. The men drew into a group behind him, watching through the saloon windows while Stagg lifted Kurt's limp body to the back of the brown Arabian and tied him into the saddle with his own lariat, in such a manner that the outlaw could ride comfortably yet would be rendered helpless to make any attempt at escape when he should return to consciousness. Then Stagg brought big white Skater around, vaulted into his own saddle, and departed down the dusty road, leading the brown Arabian.

"These quiet ones are dangerous," sighed Swabs. "I guess it wasn't any use trying to stop Bill Stagg."

"I don't vant to stop him ven I get a goot look in his face vonce," said Pete Gulick bluntly, hitching his chaps belt up around his fat little belly. "Ve don't go messing mit Bill Stagg's bizness. Ve go home now, und ve keep quiet till ve see vot Bill's going to do. You punks tell everybody dot Bill's got Kurt, und to keep hands off till ye find out vot's up. Come on mit you!"

And the little fat Dutchman stamped out of the Idle Hour, wondering just where his top hand was going to take Kurt Quillan.

CHAPTER III

A FOOL FOR BLUE

PETE GULICK was ignorant of the fact that
Kurt's jaw was broken, or he would have known
exactly where Stagg was bound with his prisoner.
Stagg knew the jaw was broken. He had felt the
bone give under his knuckles. He had heard it
crack. Given that knowledge, there was only
one possible immediate destination. He was
bound for the home of Doctor Mordan, in
Arroyo. Arroyo lay forty miles east of Seco
Springs, more east than north, by far.

That is, the distance to Arroyo was only forty
miles if a man took a course across country. By
the road one travelled a good sixty miles in the
journey. After getting into the hills, the going
was retarded to a man's pace by either route, and
Stagg knew that fast travelling was out of the
question. A man taking a fast pace and going by
the road could arrive in Arroyo ahead of a man
travelling slowly across country. But Stagg could
not choose his pace. He was forced to ride slowly
on account of the injured gunman, so he was
compelled to take the route across country.

Before the two men had left Seco Springs a
mile behind, Quillan had regained consciousness, to find himself in a great deal of pain, of

which fact he did not leave Stagg long in ignorance. He straightened in the saddle, took stock
of his situation, and his voice rose in an even
flow of malignant curses, from which he very
shortly subsided to silence, simply because any
attempt to speak caused him too acute misery.

Stagg turned in the saddle to glance back at
him, and again there was in his deep tones that
something which might have been an elusive
kind of pity.

"Every word you speak is only making your
jaw hurt worse, Kurt. I know that the jar of riding
makes it pretty tough for you, even as slow as
we're going, but shut up and take it with the best
grace you can! I didn't mean to break your jaw. I
hit harder than I intended to, because I didn't
want any gun play, and I had to be sure to knock
you out. I'm getting you as fast as I can to Doc
Mordan." Kurt's face was swelling and turning
black. Stagg didn't like that. As soon as they
reached Seco Springs Creek, he thought, he
would see what cold water would do. It ought to
keep the swelling down and ease the pain some.

Quillan attempted no answer. He was too badly
ridden by pain to give much consideration to
anything but the desire for relief. He had never
been badly hurt before. Intense pain was a new
thing to him. He had never been thrown by an
obstreperous broncho hard enough to be more
than slightly bruised. He had never been really

sick of any disease. No man's bullet had ever even so much as scored his flesh. But he knew pain now, and he was dizzy from the effects of it. His head was one solid unceasing ache. His face had begun to feel hot and stiff. He was unpleasantly sick at his stomach. The sun was blistering his shoulders and back, the relentless heat of its direct rays doubled his misery, and the two men could take little advantage of passing areas of shade.

That pent incandescent force was no less potent in him; it was merely insulated by the dull coating of his misery.

At Seco Springs Creek Stagg called a halt, soaked his neckerchief in the icy mountain stream, and tried to alleviate the outlaw's pain with the cold water application. Kurt only groaned a curse and turned his head away; and Stagg decided that any alleviating measures possible to him were too crude and too few, his ignorance of broken jaws too profound, for any waste of time to be condoned. His one expedient was to get Quillan to the doctor with all possible speed. So he set all his thoughts and effort to that course.

Dusk had fallen by the time the two men came at last to Arroyo. Stagg himself was weary, and Quillan was stupid and groggy with fever.

The dusk had deepened to early night when Stagg at last brought the two horses to a halt discreetly in Mordan's back yard. The yard, under the spreading shade trees, was only a pool of shadow. No answer came to Stagg's knock. Mordan was not at home. Stagg untied the help-less Kurt, lifted him from the saddle, and carried him into Mordan's living-room office. He was forced to feel his way carefully into the doctor's bedroom, locate the bed and shove a chair out of the way with his foot, before he could lay Quillan down.

He groped for a lamp, lighted it, and carried it to the small round table at the head of the bed. He removed Quillan's black leather chaps, his belts and his boots, and heaped them on the floor at the foot of the bed, lifting Quillan's feet onto the bed and straightening his body. He laid the blue beaver hat on the bureau. Quillan's eyes were closed, and he was groaning faintly in pain. Stagg, wondering just what to do next, went out into Mordan's front room, which was living room and office and reception room all three, lighted another lamp, and looked about for something that would apprise him of Mordan's whereabouts.

The doctor usually left word there when he was called away, giving information as to his destination and the expected hour of his return, for the benefit of any one who might need to get in touch with him. When Stagg swung open the front door, he found what he sought, held to the outside of the front door by a carpet tack.

Stagg drew the door back till the lamplight fell upon the note scrawled in Mordan's fine, precise handwriting. It said briefly:

Back at seven-thirty,
MORDAN.

Stagg looked across at the doctor's desk clock as he closed the door, leaving the note where it was. The hour was nine-fifteen. Mordan had intended to return before dark. Evidently he'd been delayed, which was no new thing for the doctor. The note made no mention of his place of call, so there was no way of telling where to look for him. Stagg went back to the room where Quillan lay, his anxiety increasing with every passing moment. The gunman had not moved, nor had his half delirious attempts at muttering ceased.

Stagg frowned uneasily, walked into the front room again, and stood staring at the door, wondering if he should take a chance on trying to locate Mordan.

Then he heard the doctor's buckboard draw up before the front yard, and he heaved a sigh of relief as he hurried to swing back the outer door to allow the lamp's glow to fall on the sidewalk leading from the road, and light the doctor in.

Mordan was a slim man, very tall, but stooped from the shouldering of the years and the demands of his profession. His hair was grey, his eyes were grey, and the cropped moustache on his lip was nearly white. He was a man of delicacy and gentleness, which he tried to hide under bluff tones and harsh words that did not at all make the concealment he expected of them. He came into sight of the man in the doorway now, and Stagg's black eyes widened a little in surprise.

Mordan advanced into the lamplight, along his sidewalk, carrying a suitcase in one hand, and with the other hand guiding a slender young woman over the moss-grown flagging. The doctor peered into the house as he came up the steps, wondering who was in need of him now, and smiled a quick welcome as he recognized Stagg.

"Oh, it's Bill! How are you, boy? Somebody sick over at the Circle G? Sorry to keep you waiting but I went to the station to meet my niece, and the damned train was nearly two hours late. It was due at seven-fifteen. Never is on time. Makes me tired. This is my niece, Rosanna Blue, never called anything but Micky." Mordan set the suitcase down and closed the front door.

"Micky, this is Bill Stagg, one of the best boys we've got out here."

"Micky" was tall for a girl, but she was compelled to look up to Bill's height. She gave him a quick, inclusive glance, and she liked what she saw, and smiled. She was blonde, and white-

33

skinned, and her eyes were the colour of amber. She extended a slim hand, with impulsive friendliness.

"You should say 'welcome home,' Bill. I'm not merely here for a vacation. My mother died, and I've come to live with Uncle Dan."

"Oh!" Some of Stagg's weariness and anxiety stilled, his natural male instinct toward the admiration of gentle womanhood arrested at the mere sight of Micky Blue, and he gripped her cool hand in his big fingers, smiling in return. "Then I'll say it. Welcome home, Micky. Excuse me if I turn to business, will you?"

He released her hand with the same muscular co-ordination that had set the whisky glass on the bar without a sound, and swerved his gaze to Mordan. "No, nobody's sick on the Circle G, doc. But you'd better go into the bedroom and see what you can do for Kurt Quillan. I'm afraid he's in a bad way. I knocked him down and broke his jaw."

Mordan's long thin frame started. "Kurt Quillan! Humphf! Why didn't you break his neck?"

"I have use for him, or maybe I would have. I didn't do it purposely. I only meant to knock him out. His face is swelling, turning black, he's pretty hot with fever. It happened over nine hours ago. Don't let him die, will you?"

Mordan's grey brows ridged over his slate-grey eyes in a frown. As Swabs and the ranch hands in the Idle Hour had done, he sensed some personal equation existent between Quillan and Stagg. He heard it in the tone of Stagg's voice, he saw it in the depths of Stagg's black eyes. He did not make articulate his thoughts. He had learned forty years ago that a doctor must only too often work in the dark and refrain from asking questions. He began removing his coat and vest quickly.

"No, I won't let him die. A man doesn't often die of a broken jaw, Bill. Get a hot fire in the stove, Bill, as quickly as you can. Micky, you take off your hat and jacket and put on that rubber apron hanging yonder. Get some water to heat in that white enamel pan you'll find in the kitchen by the sink; fill it clear up. See those instruments in the second tray in the cabinet? Get them to boiling for me as quickly as possible. There may be some bone splinters to remove. Bring in that tray with the tape and gauze on it when you come. Move fast, now; both of you. I'm going in to look at Kurt."

He found the gunman quite stupid with the fever that had claimed him, and easily manageable. There were but two bone splinters to remove. While Mordan was working on the injured jaw, Micky stood quietly by, ready with whatever assistance she might be able to give. Stagg stood across the bed, huge and still, looking down at Kurt. He spoke to the doctor without raising his gaze.

35

"I'll tell you what I told the boss, and the boys in the Idle Hour, doc. Kurt's killing days are over. I'm taking charge of him from now on. The reason back of that action is something I don't care to talk about. I haven't anything more to say."

Mordan lifted his penetrating grey eyes, as he laid the second bone splinter in a small enamel tray. "I guess that's enough, Bill. My curiosity always has been healthy, but reasonably obedient to my dictates." His gaze shifted to his niece. "Pretty rough on you, to drop right into things like this, Micky, but I knew you'd rather be in on the job than stand around doing nothing. This is a kind of special case, you know; a kind of special patient." His light dry voice took on a sardonic tinge. "You remember on the way over from the station I told you we had a real gunman running loose over the Seco? Well, Quillan is it."

"Oh, yes? The fellow who just killed the foster father who had brought him up?" Micky's eyes dropped to Quillan's discoloured face, in quick, new interest. "I begin to understand the veiled remarks passing between you and Bill, now. So, that's your gunman and outlaw! He looks like something out of a romantic lady's dreams. I suppose there really is no danger of his dying?"

"I'm afraid not," answered Mordan dryly. "He's pretty sick from the injury, his fever's pretty high; but that was aggravated by his riding so far in the hot sun without anything being done for him. But there was no way of evading that. I'm the only doctor on the Seco, and Bill got him here as quickly as it could have been done with consideration for the fellow's injury. Quillan will be all right. He'll have a few days of hurting, though. Nasty fracture. You come around here and hold his hand for me, Bill, so he can't move suddenly and break the needle. I'm going to give him another shot before I go on. Have to set the jaw, and wire those teeth. It's going to be bad if he comes out of his stupor."

In spite of the alleviating influence of the hypodermic injection, the severe pain jerked Kurt to consciousness, and he stared up at Mordan, wild agony clouding that clean cold blue of his eyes. The blue eyes moved to Stagg, who had come around the end of the bed to assist with the hypodermic, and was still standing there by the doctor. Stagg leaned over the bed, and laid one big hand on Quillan's shoulder in a tight commanding grip.

"Take it easy, Kurt. The doctor is going to be through with this business in a few minutes now."

Mordan's probing gaze flicked over Stagg's face, curious, calculating, but he spoke to his niece. "Get me that can of ether on that shelf, Micky. We'll have to put him to sleep. No, that bigger can to the right. That's it. Thanks. And the pad of cotton. Now, Kurt, you breathe deep. This will put you out so you won't feel a thing, and when you wake up it will be all over. Come on, now. Breathe it in."

Quillan, objecting much more to the pain than he did to the thought of the anæsthetic, obeyed, strangled a little over the ether, lifted a groping hand, and relaxed, flaccid, into unconsciousness again. Mordan worked rapidly, while Micky administered the ether, and Stagg looked on silent and absorbed by his thoughts.

Within a short time the job was done, the teeth and bone held in place by silver wire, the broken jaw bandaged, and all evidence of the messy task removed. With a medicine dropper, the doctor dripped into the unconscious man's mouth a palliative for the fever, turned down the light, and motioned Stagg and Micky into the other room.

A smile of approval lighted Mordan's thin face, as he gazed at his niece, rolled down his sleeves and lounged into a chair. "I must commend your adaptability, Micky. You stood up to it like a veteran. I wouldn't have been surprised at you if you'd fainted on me there when it got mussy. But you worked right through the job as if you'd been trained to it."

"I have been trained to it, Uncle Dan. I've been working in a doctor's office for three years. I'm used to things like that." The girl's gaze, speculative, veiled, provocative with a slight cast of hostility, turned to brood on Stagg's face. "I think that easing the suffering of others is about as noble a work as any one can choose, whether the people you doctor are good or bad. That's why I chose it. Only—it has always seemed so inconsistent, so futile, to me, to minister to a man, to heal his injuries, merely so that he can recover and you can hang him."

Stagg rose to the challenge in words and tone. "Nobody's going to hang him." His gaze brooded, also, on the delicate contours of her face made golden by the lamplight, on the clean curve of her throat, on the shimmering silver lights that followed the waves and troughs in her pale blond hair. "That's why I barged in and took command of this situation myself. I knew the boys would hang him if I didn't stop them. And —how is a man going to square things that have gotten all twisted up if you simply break his neck and stick him under the dirt? That's another brand of inconsistency, if you ask me."

"Seventeen years is a long time," said the doctor, but he did not look at Bill Stagg, and he seemed to be insinuating that somebody had already had seventeen years to square something that had gotten all twisted up and hadn't done a very good job of it.

"Not long enough for some people to forget in," replied Bill Stagg. "Don't begin guessing, doc. Because you're sure to guess wrong. And there are some things that nobody knows. I'm on their trail. I'm not talking about them yet. Perhaps I never will do any talking about them—and then, again, maybe I will. It all depends on what I can dig up, and I haven't found the places to dig yet. How long do you think Kurt will have to stay here before I can take him away?"

"I couldn't say definitely, Bill. If everything goes as it should, he'll probably be cursing you between his teeth to-morrow morning. The fever will likely be gone in a day or two. Oh, I expect you'll be able to take him along in less than a week. Get all the liquid nourishment down him that you can until I dare remove those wires so he can open his jaws." The doctor's gaze abruptly shifted to Micky's face. "What's the matter, Micky? You've a queer look in your eyes."

The wide eyes, so like dark unsmoky amber, fixed on the doctor's thin, wind-seamed visage. "I was thinking of that man in there on your bed, Uncle Dan; of the queer things you and Bill are saying, of the terrible things Kurt Quillan has done. There is something about him that is—oh, I don't know—sad is the word, I guess. He's very handsome, isn't he?"

"Handsome?" Mordan's thin frame roused in his chair. "Yes, he's a handsome devil all right, if you like them hard-grained and ruthless. But don't you go getting any romantic ideas about that fellow, Miss Micky. He's a killer, and a low one. There's nothing in him to admire. He's bad clean through."

Micky shook her head, the brooding look still in her amber gaze. "No. He is not bad clean through, Uncle Dan. You're exaggerating the extent of his degeneration, intentionally, perhaps. He is only partly bad. Maybe he'd never have been bad at all, if he'd had his way about it, Doctor Mordan."

"I wonder if you could be right about that?" Was that hope in Bill Stagg's face? Was that the look of a man drowning and catching at a straw? "He's bad. He's lower than a snake's belly. I wouldn't be guilty of pulling any sob stuff in defence of Kurt Quillan. But—you know that saying about people being great? I suppose you could twist it to apply to people being bad, too, like this: some people are born killers, some achieve the status of killers, and some have killing thrust upon them. I wish I could believe that Kurt had killing thrust upon him. Don't ask me why. It's a long story. But I'm promising you and the doctor that Kurt will never go blood-spilling again if I can help it. And if I can't help it, I'll kill him myself. And I never shot at a man yet."

"Bill." Mordan drew his thin body erect, and the expression on his lined face was not curiosity; it was intense interest born of concern. "How did you know where Kurt was, and how did you manage to get hold of him?"

Stagg told him, concisely and completely, and Mordan nodded. "I see. But, if Louie was scared out of his pants, as you told the boys in Seco Springs, how did you persuade him to go close enough to Kurt Quillan to speak to him?"

"Do you like Lispy Louie, doc?"

"No! How could I?"

"How many other people feel the same way?"

"Everybody that ever knew him, I guess."

"You're likely right, doc. Do you suppose Louie knows it?"

"He'd have to know it, Bill. Say, what the devil are you getting at?"

"Well, doc, I don't like him either. But there's some damn fool thing in me that is sorry for the misfits and the incompetents. I have to be kind to them. I go out of my way to be kind to them. As you plant flowers. And Lispy has got the idea that I like him. I wouldn't disabuse his mind of the error for money. So, who would he go to, when he was scared pink and wanted help?"

"I see. And he managed the courage to go up and speak to Kurt for the same reason. But Kurt is a natural woodsman. It would be practically impossible to take him by surprise in the woods. I can't understand how he ever exposed himself long enough for Louie to get sight of him and know he was there. Freakish train of circumstances, Bill. If Louie hadn't got sight of Kurt by some strange chance, he wouldn't have been frightened, he wouldn't have come to you, you wouldn't have known where Kurt was so that you could dare him into your trap, and the posse would have eventually found him, and he'd be a dead man by now. I'd give a lot to know how he made the error of letting Lispy Louie get sight of him."

"So would I, but I'm not going to ask him." Stagg rose to his feet, stretching to his astounding height. "Well, I guess I'll run along. I'll stay over at Stokes's till Kurt's well enough to travel again. I'm certainly glad you came here, Micky. Rain in the desert. I'll be back in the morning to see how Kurt is. Good night."

Micky sat very still for a long moment, gazing at the door which closed after Stagg as he went out, and neither she nor the doctor spoke till the big man's footsteps had died away in the night. Then the girl turned her gaze upon her uncle, to see that he was watching her with a quizzical smile.

"People—people!" she said sombrely. "How they hurt, how they hope, and what strange and frenzied things they do! You and Bill have roused my curiosity. I'm ready to give a good deal, too, to learn whatever gave your Lispy Louie a chance to know that Quillan was in his neighbourhood. Tell me more about this business, Uncle Dan. Who is Lispy Louie?"

The doctor told her. He described Louie and

his Crazy L Ranch with the terse directness that doctors learn to employ. When he had finished, she nodded, and smiled.

"Does he lisp, really?"

"Badly."

"Queer little man, isn't he? What strange under-currents are here, Uncle Dan? Why are you so astounded at Bill Stagg's taking possession of Quillan as he has already done?"

Mordan scowled and shook his head, not in negation, but as a man does who strives to clear his senses. "I don't really know, Micky. There's something queer in it, and no mistake. Seventeen years ago Lem Strickland found Kurt's mother, Bess Quillan, dead in Lobo Pass. Shot twice, once through the head. Lobo Pass is north-east of here, about ninety miles, beyond the Seven Up Ranch. Kurt was then about four years old, as near as Lem could guess, and he was huddled by his mother's body, crying. Lem took the dead woman to his ranch, and buried her. He kept the boy and brought him up. He was single then. He married Mrs. Strickland about five years after he brought the boy from Lobo Pass. That's all anyone ever has known about it."

"Did Bill Stagg know Strickland well?"

"Only slightly, as one of the Seco ranchers. I know that. And you heard Bill himself admit that Kurt didn't know Bill from Adam's off ox. You know as much about the strange undercurrents as I do, Micky, because now you know all that I know about the whole business. Well, you'd better get to bed, young lady. You've had a long ride and you must be tired. Come on and I'll show you to the room I got ready for you. I'll sit up a while and watch Kurt. He's in my bed."

Micky voiced a prompt remonstrance. "I'm not tired, Uncle Dan. You're the one who's tired. And you haven't any intention of just watching Quillan for a little while, either. You mean to stay up all night, and you know it. A broken jaw isn't enough to lay a man flat for long, and Quillan is a killer, and you're appointing yourself jailer and guard. You aren't going to chance his getting up and making an escape."

Mordan laughed. "Check! What of it?"

"You're the one who's tired, I said. That's what of it. You go to bed in my room and get some sleep now while he's groggy from fever and the ether. I'll sit up and watch. I've done aplenty of night watching by patients. If he shows the least sign of returning consciousness, I'll call you. That's a promise."

"All right," Mordan agreed. "If you're not sleepy. I'll admit that I am pretty tired. I had a couple of hard cases to-day. But before I go to bed I'll just tie Kurt's hands and feet so he can't do any damage if he does wake up. I wouldn't trust that snake not to kill his own grandmother. And, although I can't see what good he'd be to anybody, if Bill wants him, he's going to be right here waiting when Bill comes to get him."

So the doctor tied Kurt Quillan into his bed, hand and foot, placing the unconscious man in no discomfort, but binding him so efficiently that he couldn't even rise to a sitting position when he did return to consciousness. Then Mordan went to seek a little rest, leaving the girl sitting near the outlaw's bedside, with a magazine in her lap. But she did not then read anything in the magazine. Nurses are interested in their patients, even if the patients don't always think so. And this was a patient whose kind was new to her experience.

Yet all her speculation and wondering concerning him were set at naught. He was only an unconscious form lying on a bed, his cold blue eyes closed, his chestnut hair burning in one spot where the lamplight touched it, his pent and vibrant force curtained from her by the veil of fever and anæsthesia that drifted foglike between her and his alert brain, his swift and facile intelligence.

She wondered what dark and devious trail twisted back in to the years, to that shrouded night in Lobo Pass, where Lem Strickland had found a dead woman and a terrorized child; and where that trail would lead from here on. She wondered, too, if there might not be a better and brighter trail for him if someone could turn his feet toward it. Men as hardened and sinister as

46

Kurt Quillan did sometimes turn to better and brighter ways, if they were not already warped in the moulding. She believed that, simply because she liked to believe in the basic goodness of men. She liked to believe in redemption, though she knew of those two ways, atonement or death, and she knew that it sometimes took both of them to accomplish the redemption.

She found herself wishing that he would waken, and look at her, that she might glimpse something of the spirit that dwelt in the recumbent and inert figure. She noted rather sharply the blue beaver hat, the blue shirt, the dark blue wool trousers. And suddenly he opened his eyes, and gazed straight into her face, and she spoke the thought that was in her mind.

"You like blue, don't you?"

He was conscious of his dizziness more than his pain. He was fully aware of her presence for the first time. Only those who have reacted from anæsthesia and pain can know how he felt. And he answered without stopping to weigh his utterance, speaking the truth.

"I do. I don't care what colour anything is so long as it's blue. I'm a fool for blue. If I weren't, I wouldn't be here with a broken jaw."

She ignored whatever cryptic reason lay behind that statement. She rose and stepped to the head of the bed. "Just lie perfectly quiet, please. If you move about you're liable to make yourself sick.

47

We want to avoid that. It would be frightfully unpleasant for you. You haven't eaten anything for nine hours, and that is going to help a great deal."

He muttered painfully, through his closed teeth. "I haven't eaten for over twenty hours. Are you a nurse?"

"Yes. I'm Doctor Mordan's niece."

"What's the matter with my mouth? I can't open it."

"No. Your jaws are wired shut. So the bone can knit properly. Don't try to talk any more."

"O.K. I'll just lie here and look at you." He glanced down at the ropes that bound him, and a twisted leer of a smile lifted the corner of his mouth opposite the broken jaw. "Any objection to that?"

She felt then the first reaction of the force that burned within him. It quivered behind his surface of dearly-bought nonchalance, in the eyes of cold, clean blue that she saw opened wide for the first time. She answered slowly:

"None. I don't believe that will hurt you. It never has hurt any of my patients yet. I'll tell you about your jaw, if you care to know."

"Go ahead." So she told him all there was to tell, and when she had finished, she smiled. On the side of his mouth opposite the bandage the one visible dimple drove the colour away, and left the little white spot for an instant where the dimple had been.

She said almost sharply: "What were you doing to let that Lispy Louie get sight of you so that he could tell anyone where you were?"

He had closed his eyes. At that question he opened them, and their cold blue gaze centred on her face. "I was picking violets."

The tone was mocking, so insolent that it was almost an insult, and she shrank and straightened in the same movement. She said curtly: "Don't talk any more. I'll give you some water if you want it. You may have a little if you don't feel nauseated."

"No, thanks. I don't feel sick, but I don't want any water. I'll just lie here and look at you." But the cold blue eyes closed, and unconsciousness claimed him yet again.

At midnight, he roused again, and though he knew she was there he made no attempt to address her. She drowsed in her chair, and at a little after dawn Mordan found them there, both asleep. He wakened the girl and commanded tersely that she go to bed and rest. She rose from her chair, stiffly, stretching her cramped muscles, and followed the doctor into the office living-room.

"Uncle Dan," she asked, nudged both by a formless indignation and by curiosity, "if you asked any of these men out here about something and he said he'd been picking violets, what would you gather that he meant?"

Mordan smiled thinly. "It's not an uncommon phrase with these boys out here, my dear. They'd be telling you mildly to mind your own business. Go to bed, will you?"

CHAPTER IV

THE DEVIOUS HEART

KURT QUILLAN woke from sleep with a lessening of the feeling of dizziness and stupor. From the slit of his half closed eyes he saw the doctor standing in the doorway talking in a subdued undertone to his niece. The outlaw's sickness had passed. He was beginning to be conscious of hunger. The pain lingered, rather fiercely. His head still ached from chin to crown, and his jaw was a misery, and his stomach demanded something to alleviate its emptiness.

But, stronger than the hunger, was a calculating consideration of the most feasible manner in which he might accomplish escape.

Nothing seemed to present itself either as advisable or acceptable. For a full hour he explored every idea worthy of the effort, and he was no further ahead. Then Micky came tiptoeing into the room, and found him awake, and went out again without a word, to fetch a bowl of creamed soup that held nourishment as well as some slight appeasing for his hunger.

He made no attempt to speak. She said little, save to advise him to take the soup and realize its value to his condition, and she fed it to him with a spoon, but there was a restraint in her gaze and air. She was still smarting under his reproof, his telling her, as Mordan had explained, to mind her own business.

When he had swallowed the last spoonful of the creamed soup, he asked abruptly:

"Where did Bill Stagg go? Did he give you any idea what he wants of me?"

Micky rose in her chair, the empty bowl in her hand. "I—no. He gave us no idea what he wants of you. He said he would be staying at Stokes's —wherever that is. Would you like some water now?"

"No, thanks." The life that was in him was again quivering close to the surface, and he was occupied for the moment with a feeling of scorn for his own past lack of wariness and alertness to danger. The china bowl in her hands was blue, and he gazed at it, absently, and managed a short, hard laugh. "Pretty bowl. Blue. I suppose all men are fools over something. Here I lie, with a broken jaw and a headache, because I can't resist anything that's blue. If I hadn't gone out into the clear to pick those damned violets just because they made such a bright-blue patch there on the creek bank, I wouldn't have been where Louie le Grande could see me—and I wouldn't be here."

Micky had started to leave the room, but she stopped at that last sentence, and turned to look down at him with a blend of surprise and disbelief.

"Do you mean to say you were really picking violets?"

The gunman managed another hard curt laugh. "Yes, beautiful lady. I was picking violets. Did you think I said that merely to put you off? You know, they were so awfully blue; entirely lacking in that purplish shade wild violets often have, and it's late in the year for them. The only place you'll see them now is up in the mountains. And I'd been riding through such colourless country for miles. They were like a little blue funeral wreath on the creek bank. My funeral, maybe."

"Well, did you have to go into Seco Springs merely because of the message Bill Stagg sent you?" asked Micky.

"Yes. I'm afraid I had to." The mocking voice muted. "I'm the kind of cockeyed mortal who picks violets and can't take a dare."

"Very well, then. I dare you to stop trying to talk and make some attempt to keep quiet. I apologize for being the cause of your talking at all. Doctor Mordan said you weren't to do it."

"It will take more than Doctor Mordan and a broken jaw to keep me from talking when I have anything to say. And it would take more than a little dizziness and a headache to keep me from thinking, when I have anything to think about.

And a man would have plenty to think about when you're around."

"Then I'll go out in the other room," said Micky curtly.

And she did; and told Mordan that Quillan would talk, though her curiosity was partly to blame for it, and she knew that was inexcusable and she was sorry.

Mordan's grey eyes twinkled at her. "It won't kill him. But keep him as quiet as you can. Tell him a bedtime story or something. And don't ask him what his grandmother's name was, because I don't think he knows." Which was mild reproof, and she regretted being deserving of it.

To make up for her own lapse, she went in and sat down in the chair by Kurt's bed, without saying a word. She found that he had gone to sleep.

When he wakened, she was not in the room, but on the table by the head of the bed was a half-pint squat jar, and the jar was overflowing with tiny bright-blue flowers. The outlaw lay quiescent, gazing at them. They were such a brilliant, shining blue. He knew the girl had put them there. He didn't remember ever having seen that kind of flower before.

The heart of Kurt Quillan was a devious mechanism. His brain was of that same character. That he had adopted cunning and duplicity in desperation was something no man knew.

Both qualities had become dangerously close to acquiring the fixed status of habit, so that now, with the dawning light of an idea that might prove workable, they added their approval and abetment. Since both pain and dizziness had abated, he had known no thought save the concealed but consuming desire for escape. Up to now no feasible avenue of escape had presented itself—not until he wakened from his doze and saw the jar of blue flowers standing there on the small round table.

Then the idea was born almost full blown. He must have caught the girl's personal interest. She must have been touched, as women, being plastic, could be touched, by what he had said of the violets and his passion for the colour blue. He hadn't recounted it with any object of gaining such a reaction; he had merely told the truth, with an inward sneer for his own gullibility; but he saw that he had gained that reaction all the same. And the idea was born: he might use the girl as a fulcrum to lever himself out of this predicament.

It was certainly worth cultivating, that idea. It grew on him the more he thought of it, so that when Micky came tiptoeing back into the room to see whether he still slept, he was watching her face and listening to the tone of her voice from then on, coolly weighing the extent of whatever personal impression he might have made, and striving with all his shrewdness to foster it.

He gestured with one of his bound hands toward the jar of blue flowers. "Where did they come from?"

Faint surprise widened her gaze. "Why, haven't you seen Uncle Dan's yard?"

"I haven't. I've never spent much time around Arroyo. I've never been near this house till last night, and we reached here after dark. What are they?"

"Lobelia." Micky seated herself in the chair by the bed. "One of the bluest flowers in the world. Out in Uncle Dan's front yard, there is a little stone wall running all the way across the front edge of the lot, not more than two feet high. All along the top, the wall is hollow for about ten inches down. The hollow is filled with earth. The whole top of the wall is a mass of lobelia. And he has some in the porch boxes along the porch front. He's always loved flowers. The front yard is full of them, but the lobelia are the only blue ones. So I brought them in for you to look at."

No, he couldn't be mistaken. The expression of her amber eyes was clear. Personal interest was there, and a woman's pity and a kind of grudging admiration. The idea was very clearly worth all the play he could give it. If she were fool enough to be captured by the fascination of a handsome face, and the romantically intriguing figure of a bad man with a mysterious history, it was all water on the mill wheel for him. And the faster he could make the mill grind, the quicker he could be free from this intolerable predicament.

He lay there and gazed at her, trying to judge with cold calculation just how far he dared go. He had felt no instinct to response at recognition of her interest in him, which he had misread completely, because it was merely humane concern, partly clinical and partly compassionate. It mattered little to him how he gained freedom from the doctor's vigilant detention, and thereby gained also opportunity to strike back at Stagg. If he could accomplish it via an unsuspected surprise manœuvre, through the collusion of an impressionable girl, he could think of no way to engineer it with less danger of failure. As a matter of fact, very probably that was about the only way in which he would be able to manage escape, since he was without his guns or an opportunity to rely on them if he had them.

He wasted no thought or concern as to how such an eventuality might boomerang on the girl: he had neither much use for nor interest in girls, and this one was no exception. She was a tool to his need, and nothing more. Stagg had, after all, played into his hands by bringing him here where there was an impressionable girl to be bent to his machinations. He would remember to taunt Stagg with that, just before he blew his brains out. And he continued to gaze at the brilliant blue lobelia, and his voice softened as if he himself were touched by her act.

"Do I say thank you?"

"Yes. By keeping still. I've already committed the unpardonable act of leading you to talk when the doctor said for you not to do it."

He gave her the half smile that was all he could manage with his stiff and swollen face, and in spite of herself her eyes held fascinated on the dimple that drove the colour from the uninjured corner of his mouth.

"Don't blame yourself. You couldn't prevent my talking. I told you that. Your memory's pretty short, isn't it? Do you know, you're different from any girl I ever knew?"

Micky repressed a frown, and her amber eyes were deep and sober. "Am I? You're different from any of the men I ever knew, too. Yet, you're like everybody else, after all. You're human enough to think you have to deliver what others expect of you, whether you really feel like doing it or not."

The sardonic smile died out of the cold-blue eyes. "Yes? And what do you mean by that? That sounds like a nasty crack."

"Perhaps it is. I meant it for one, anyway. You've killed a few people and gotten yourself a reputation as a bad man. You've put up a bluff of really feeling like a bad man, because people expected it of you, till you're dangerously close to becoming as bad as people think you are. But you're not all bad. I'm certain of that. I wish I could be the means of helping you never to want to do anything low or vicious again. You have an astounding force. You could be anything you wanted to be, Kurt Quillan."

He was a little startled. Her tone was too steady, too sincere, the light of her sombre eyes too penetrating in their scrutiny, to be brushed aside lightly. He refused to pause for any analysis of his own unexpected reactions. His voice sharpened. "You're going a little far in your attempts at reform, lady. I've killed seven men, you know; eight, with Lem Strickland."

"Yes, I know. That seems to have been the worst thing you ever did. Just why did you shoot Mr. Strickland, anyway?"

"He damned well deserved it, just as all the other seven did. However, I didn't mean to kill Lem, no matter what he had done. That may not make me a bad man, but it doesn't make me any sweet-scented lily, either. I suppose you'll tell me there's even redemption for a shunk like me."

The girl's intent gaze did not waver. A small smile lifted her sober mouth. "You see, I told you you were perilously close to becoming the real thing. You said that in the same spirit you came swaggering into Seco Springs to show other men you wouldn't take a dare. It doesn't impress me. Yes, there's redemption for men like you; there's redemption for any man; two ways of redemption, Kurt. Absolution for any sin. By living and atoning, or by dying and wiping the slate clean. And even if it takes both, it's worth it; because there's no percentage in making a fool of yourself."

One can hit a man between the eyes, or on the chin, or over the heart, and lay him out; by which you can cause him pain, and fury, or fear, or the lust for retaliation. But no physical blow ever struck can bruise a man so hard or sting so long as the verbal blow that hits him fairly on his weak spot, which was the sort of blow Micky had delivered to Kurt Quillan in those crisp words. And she got up and walked out of the room, so that they could sink in, and he wouldn't be tempted to talk any more.

For at least two hours, he lay there alternately staring at the blue lobelia and thinking, or lay with closed eyes thinking. It took him fully that long to recover from that clean uppercut and get his thinking processes straight again. And the almost viciously cold conclusion he reached was that if she thought he was putting up a bluff, he would show her what a real bluff was. Only, she wouldn't know it for a bluff till afterward—after he was gone, blazing his way out of Arroyo with both guns, and she had to remember that she was the one who had been duped by his smooth pretence into turning him loose.

He was still occupied with that highly entrancing train of thought when Stagg walked into the room in company with Mordan, to see how he was feeling. The outlaw began his bluff right then; because he wanted to put it over as rapidly as possible, and Micky was standing there looking on and listening. The blue eyes were burning again with that fire which blurred their clean colour.

"You certainly laid me out, Bill. But I'm holding no grudge. I'm thanking you instead— for saving my neck. Doc says I'm coming along better than he expected."

Mordan's thin face was noncommittal, his grey eyes wary. "You certainly are. You've scarcely any fever left, and it's still going down when it would be coming up if it was going to rise again. If you continue this way, you can go with Stagg in two or three days. It will be up to you then to take care of yourself and let nature complete the healing. There won't be anything more I can do but take the wires off in a couple of weeks."

"All right, I'll go along then." Stagg's black eyes lingered on the lithe blue-clad body lying bound to the bed. "I'll wait over at Stokes's, and as soon as doc says you can leave, we'll light out." He turned from the bed and quitted the room, and Mordan followed him out of the house onto the front porch, where the blue lobelia blazed like blue flame all along the porch boxes.

"I don't know just what to make of him, Bill," the doctor said. "Either you've scared the daylights out of him, or he's had a change of heart."

Stagg laughed. "He's had no change of heart. Black doesn't change to white over night. And when the devil begins singing hymns—look out. Keep your eye on him, and if he makes a suspicious move crack him over the head and send for me. I never heard of a rattlesnake turning into a pussycat yet."

"Great minds do run in the same channel, don't they?" Mordan's grey eyes twinkled. "He won't get very far if he's trying to pull a fast one, Bill. Don't worry. I'm watching him."

The doctor, in the sixty-nine years he had lived, had learned to control his facial muscles so that they lied smoothly or told the truth suavely, at his command. Yet in Kurt Quillan he dealt with a man who had put in some intensive training in watching the expressions of other men's faces. Kurt was aware of the exact extent of the doctor's surveillance. He knew that his one possible period of escape must be at night while the doctor slept. He knew that the girl was far more mature and discerning than he had given her credit for being. If he was to succeed with the bluff he planned, he must make it a good one. When Mordan and Stagg left the room, he turned upon her his temporarily one-sided smile.

"I'm licked. I quit. Where do we go from here?"

She reseated herself and picked up the magazine that lay on the floor by her chair. "I would suggest that you go back to the first man you killed, and start the recapitulation there. And when you've got the entire score tallied, go away to some other part of the country and build yourself a better and brighter trail. That is, if you can ever make yourself believe that rehabilitation and regeneration are worth the effort. Now keep still; I'm going to read."

"I'll keep still if you'll read aloud." Not that he particularly cared about any magazine story, but that he wanted to keep her there, to persist in fostering the deception he wanted her to accept as a truth. She chose deliberately the thing she read; a character study of a man who never really had any particular yearning to be a bad man, but who never had the stamina to defeat his own weaknesses, either, and who ended by hanging from the limb of a poplar tree.

She started upon another story, but the gentle monotone of her voice put him to sleep. She went softly from the room and lay down on her own bed to sleep against the night watch to come.

Mordan took up the post of watcher in the adjoining room, in such a position that he could see the bed where Kurt lay. The doctor went about quietly getting his own meal at noon, then went back to his watch.

Kurt woke twice, but Mordan did not speak to him, and he went back to sleep. The girl slept till the doctor had a meal prepared and woke her to share it. After the dinner, she went in to feed her patient strong broth, and milk, and stout coffee enriched by thick cream.

It was thin fare, but it held nourishment, and he relished the strengthened glow he felt after it. He asked her to read to him again, and she did it, willingly. He asserted that he had slept so much all day, he was wakeful now. She had expected that, as a matter of course. He listened, his eyes closed most of the time, till she finished reading, then he said, as if she had but the moment before counselled him to build that brighter and better trail in a new land.

"Just how far do you think I'll get, trying to start over or leave the Seco range, if I lie here until Stagg comes to take me away like a bound cur?"

"And so what?" she said steadily.

"And so there's only one way for me. I have to slip out of here after night, and put a lot of miles behind me, before he has any idea I'm gone."

"Are you afraid of Bill Stagg?"

"Afraid!" The blue eyes were as cold as they had ever been, then a little startled light flashed across the clear irises. For he realized that, incredible as it seemed, he was afraid of Stagg.

He had not to date experienced the unpleasant

state of being any man's helpless prisoner. The thought of being held captive by the huge man with the hard hands was abominable; he had not realized just how intolerable it was till just now.

He repeated, almost wonderingly: "Afraid. I suspect you've hit it, Micky. I'm afraid of him. Not because he's bigger than I, and I have no gun—but because I don't know who he is, and I don't know what he wants of me. I don't know what cause he has for wanting to take his temper out on me. Probably any man would shrink from paying a bill he never knew he owed."

"Listen to me, Kurt." Micky tossed the magazine to the floor, and leaned toward him in her chair, her amber eyes holding his, and she was the kind of person who could ache for the wasted beauty in his face. She was the kind of person who could weep for the loss of all potential beneficence wantonly stricken out of a world so poor in benefits and so rich in woe, but she wanted no man to see the tears. Which was a little larger brand of compassion than she had ever known to exist. "Do you think you could really want to start at scratch? Not for any human being's sake but your own. Until you can strive for your regeneration from that basic impulse, you aren't likely to get very far with it."

"Promises are cheap." His chiselled features were again that hue of craft paper, as they had been when he faced Stagg in the Idle Hour. "We're getting into pretty deep water, but I'll have to admit that if I thought there really was any way for me to sponge off the record and start a new one—well, you're right. There's no percentage in making a fool of yourself. I'm not offering any promise. Words are too easily put together. But that much I mean: if there was a chance, I'd take it. If you're in earnest about helping a man to start over, suppose you untie these ropes, slip me one of the doctor's guns, and let me fade out of the scene."

Micky straightened, and rose to her feet. "I can't untie them. The doctor has them secured too well. I'll have to get a knife and cut them. Be very quiet. Uncle Dan wakes easily. He's a light sleeper. I'll be back quickly."

"Do you know—I'll never forget this, Micky. I didn't much believe you'd do it." His eyes followed her to the door, and now they were burning again, with a little different fire than they had hitherto known.

The girl was deeper than he had dreamed she was. She was of a rare kind. She went to the heart of things, without wasting words. And she was right. He had been perilously close to believing that he was what he thought he had become. He recoiled a little to think how close. Why should a man want to live like a prowling jackal, anyway? It was more than he knew, now that he was suddenly sane again. He did not ask himself what had recalled that sanity.

He watched her go swiftly from the room. He could not hear her glide soundlessly into the doctor's room. He could not see her bend over Mordan's bed. He could not see Mordan start and sit up, nor hear the girl whisper close to his ear:

"You're right, Uncle Dan. He's dangerous. He wants me to turn him loose. He's been working for this for hours, planning toward it, little suspecting that I saw through his suave pretence. I'm going into the kitchen after a knife. Get up. Pretend you've heard something. Come in and stop me from freeing him. Let him keep the idea that I believe in him. It might be worth something—later."

Then she was gone, as silently as she had come, and Mordan slipped from his bed and slid on his bare feet to the door. There he paused, listening and watching. He saw Micky go into the kitchen, come back and enter Kurt's room with a knife in her hand.

Kurt looked up as she approached the bed. "I've been bluffing, Micky. I didn't mean it. But I do mean it now. I'll light out of this country, and start over somewhere where I'll have a chance to begin clean. I wonder if I'll ever see you again? I'd like to. I'll always see you, at that—as we see things we can't forget." And only he believed that he meant it fully now.

"Hush!" Micky bent over the bed and reached for the rope that bound his hands. "The house is still and your voice carries. You mustn't wake Uncle Dan."

"Oh, no? And why mustn't you wake me?" demanded Mordan's harsh voice from behind her. "What's going on here? Micky, what are you doing with that knife?"

Micky jerked upright and whirled, relief flashing into her face. Quillan cursed madly. When a man has come to full faith himself, he does not suspect others of duplicity. Kurt had no suspicion that Micky herself had engineered this disaster to his plan for escape. He looked at the doctor, his tall, lean body there in the doorway, his long nightshirt clinging to his thin shins. He thought that he had never so hated any man.

"What the devil does this mean?" Mordan demanded, advancing into the room. "Micky, give me that knife. And leave the room."

She seized without a backward look that opportunity for escape from the uncomfortable situation, and no one could have discerned that she was not frightened and guilty, from the look on her face. She dropped the knife into Mordan's hand and literally ran from the room. Mordan glared down at the outlaw.

"And what the devil do you mean, working on my niece's sympathy and trying to give me the slip like this? Did you think you could get away with it? I couldn't be as dumb as you must think I look, Quillan."

The dark skin of the outlaw's face suffused with fury, his eyes blazed so cold that the blue irises seemed two shades lighter; but this was not the rabid fury of an evil man thwarted in the attempt to complete some vicious intent. It was the despairing fury of an awakened man who sees an opportunity for rebirth snatched from his grasp forever.

Only, Mordan did not know Kurt Quillan; he had never seen him close at hand till Stagg had stretched him there on the bed, and it is often easy to be mistaken in the reading of a face the expressions of which are unfamiliar to your eyes.

Mordan misread that blinding fury, and Kurt's mad words did nothing to point the error.

"Damn you, Mordan! I'll kill you, and Bill Stagg, too, before—"

He got no farther. The doctor's hand swung out from behind his long, concealing nightshirt. It held a heavy revolver. The hand swung up, and down. The butt of the gun thudded on Kurt's skull. Quillan quivered, and lay still. Mordan knew just where to hit. He turned and strode from the room, his nightshirt flapping against his legs. He found Micky waiting for him in the room beyond, and he halted and slammed the gun down on the nearest piece of furniture that would hold it, which happened to be an old parlour organ.

"Go over to Jay Stokes's and call Stagg," he said furiously. "The white house right across the road, in front of the livery stable. Tell him I said to come get Kurt Quillan."

Micky nodded and hurried out of the house, and Mordan looked after her with an appreciative smile. "Smart girl," he muttered to himself. "They've got to get up before daylight to get ahead of her."

Micky dashed across the street and up the board walk that led to Stokes's house, and Stagg himself opened the door, looming mountainous against the lamplight from the room beyond.

"Why, Micky! Anything gone wrong?"

"Well, yes and no, Bill. Come get your gunman. He's been trying tricks. I don't believe it would be safe to leave him there any longer. He's a desperate man. Don't let him know I came after you. Let him believe it was Uncle Dan. He thinks I'm his friend, that I was trying to set him free. I want him to continue to think that. What is he to you, Bill? I'm not prying. I have a definite reason for asking."

Bill Stagg gazed down into the girl's tense face with a troubled frown; she looked so fragile, and yet so strong, there in the faint glow of the lamplight. "I can't tell you, Micky. It may prove to be something forever better left unsaid. I'm a little slow saying things I can never take back. I'm not going to turn him loose to go killing again, if that's what you're afraid of."

"No, that isn't it, Bill." She turned to go down the steps, and Stagg closed the door and fell into step with her. "It's something I hesitate to express, Bill, but—give him a chance, won't you?"

"A chance for what? To reform?"

"No. He doesn't need to reform. I don't know why I feel that so strongly. Just give him a chance to be what he may want to be some day."

"What do you think I made such a play to get him in my hands for? Not to throw him away, Micky. To salvage anything that may be there to salvage. Only, I have to make sure it's there."

"Yes. Of course. I suppose that was what I meant."

They crossed the street and went into the doctor's house together. Mordan was waiting in the front room, a pair of trousers now over his nightshirt, slippers on his thin long feet. He had Kurt's chaps and belts lying in a roll on the centre table. He greeted Stagg brusquely:

"Sorry, Bill, but I don't want to keep him here any longer. If I were in the house alone, I wouldn't care. But I won't subject Micky to the kind of annoyance he can raise. He got obstreperous and I conked him. He's still out. And I yanked his boots on. He's all ready to go. Don't let him talk too much. Bring him back in two weeks, and I'll take the wires off."

"If he's still alive," said Stagg evenly, "I'll bring him. He may be under six feet of dirt by then. It's up to him. Do you want to bring him out of it before I take him?"

"He'll come out of it himself," answered Mordan shortly. "I just tapped him. Take him as he is. The sooner he's out of my house the quicker I'll feel easy."

He followed Stagg into the room where Quillan lay, and Micky followed at her uncle's elbow. The doctor's grey hair was dishevelled all over his head. His white moustache was bristling. He had the appearance of being badly upset.

Stagg strode to the bed, untied the ropes that bound the outlaw's hands, and loosed the slacked ropes the doctor had shoved out of the way in order to pull on the unconscious man's boots. As Stagg bent to lift the outlaw's inert body, Quillan opened his eyes, took in the significance of Stagg's presence, and sat up on the edge of the bed.

Something about him held them all almost transfixed, in a kind of hush, something that none of them had time to define, and only Micky recognized it for what it was. She recognized it because she was looking directly into the blue eyes that sought her face. She had seen a man's soul born once before, and she had never forgotten the sight. She put both her hands behind her, and backed slowly away, paling, and she

71

thought for an instant that she was going to faint.

Then he smiled, as she had not known he could smile. She had known though that tenderness was in him; there were the blue violets. For an interminable minute his gaze brooded on her face, and no one dared break the hush that dwelt about him like a light. Then he spoke, oblivious of every one but her:

"It still goes, lady. And I still hope I see you again some day, even if I have to take it both ways."

She knew then, beyond all doubt. If he had never spoken a sincere word to her before, he was speaking it now. No one in the room could doubt it, but only Micky knew what he meant. Her breath ached in her throat. Had she made some hideous error?

Kurt rose to his feet, the smile still lingering. He reached over and lifted the handful of blue flowers from the little squat jar. He looked at Bill Stagg and measured his chances for a break. And Stagg reached out and gripped his arm.

"No you don't, Kurt. There'll be no chance for you to get away from me, so don't overwork your brain planning one. Come on. Hand me his hat, will you, Micky?"

The girl pulled herself out of her dismayed abstraction, and took the hat from the bureau, and brought it to Stagg. He settled it on the gun-man's chestnut hair, and without another word propelled Kurt out of the room. Micky followed them, and Mordan came behind, and under his close-cropped white moustache his upper lip was wet with a fine beading of perspiration. In the front room Stagg caught up the chaps and belts lying on the table, and then for no particular reason Micky noticed that Stagg wore no gun. As Mordan stepped ahead and opened the front door, and Stagg started to push Quillan out into the night, the girl's voice rose in the tense room, almost sharp.

"Kurt; Kurt! I didn't know you meant it at all! But I wanted you to have a chance, anyway. I know, now. Remember that!"

He turned his head, and the blue eyes were deep with colour again. "I guess neither of us knew exactly where we were heading. And you were going to let me go, even when you didn't believe me! That's something I'll remember, too. Do you know any better word than good-bye?"

"Oh, no! No!" Micky's voice caught. "It means God be with you till we meet again. Good-bye, Kurt."

Stagg cleared his throat as if some painful obstruction had risen there. "Thanks, doc. Send me your bill. But there are some things we can't pay for."

"You don't owe me anything," said Mordan curtly. "This is your show. Good night, Bill."

And the two men went out, and the door closed

behind them, and the doctor turned to look at Micky, who stood taut and straight as if she were frozen and couldn't move.

"What is this?" Mordan asked sharply. "What's going on here that I don't get?"

"We've done him an irreparable wrong!" answered the girl starkly. "I should have let him go, and now it's forever too late. I'm afraid for him!"

Mordan's thin face tightened with swift anger. "Did he pull the wool over your eyes after all? He's a liar. He's a killer of the worst kind. He deserves nothing better than what he's going to get. But I can't blame you too much. He almost had me fooled for a minute."

Swift fire lighted in the girl's amber eyes. "Sometimes you're thick-witted, Uncle Dan! He fooled us both—not the way you inferred. And there in the bedroom, for a moment, you knew it!"

Mordan stared. "I apologize," he said curtly. "Let's get to bed."

CHAPTER V

LOBO PASS

QUILLAN made no protest as Stagg shoved him out into the night. He tried to see the blue lobelia in the porch boxes and the wall slots, but the thin moonlight was not sufficient to reveal them. He smelled the perfume rising from the blooms of the yard as he went down the walk with Stagg. He knew that his one chance of escaping from the huge man's hard hands lay in seeming utter docility till the sure chance should come. It had to come. He would not be fool enough to ask for maiming at the will of those hands by striving to force the break prematurely. He knew that he hadn't a chance of winning in a physical encounter with Stagg.

He submitted in silence while Stagg propelled him into Stokes's livery stable, and proceeded calmly to tie him hand and foot to the nearest upright of an open stall.

Then Stagg speedily saddled and bridled big white Skater and the beautiful Arabian, and tied the roll of Kurt's chaps and belts to the saddle on the brown horse. He loosed Quillan from the upright, tied him onto the Arabian, swung onto the white gelding, and rode off down the street passing from Arroyo, leading Kurt's mount. As the few lights still burning in Arroyo faded from sight, Kurt asked one question.

"Where are we bound, if you care to tell the truth?"

"To a little hide-out I have. In a cave in Lobo Pass."

Quillan's blue eyes stared ahead at the dim bulk that was Stagg's huge, erect body. Lobo Pass. As he had grown up, he had heard many times from both Lem and Mrs. Strickland the story of how Lem had found him and his mother there in the pass that dark night. Naturally curious, he had haunted Lobo Pass for years. He had come to have a lurking fondness for its austere beauty. He knew every bluff and stone of it from end to end. He knew of no cave. He said boldly:

"There is no cave within miles of Lobo Pass."

For a moment only the *clop-clop* of the horses' hoofs answered him. Then he heard Stagg's emotionless deep voice, drifting back from that dim bulk on the white horse ahead.

"You don't know everything about Lobo Pass, Kurt. There is a cave there, but it isn't easy to find. Talking isn't going to help your jaw. Keep still, will you? We'll take the road that cuts across the Circle G and the Seven Up, instead of going away to the north by Seco Trail. We'll reach the pass by noon tomorrow, easy."

That was a strange ride through the night and the dawn and the early morning; two grim men, each sunk in his own silence, one a captor, the other a prisoner, and each almost as confused as the other about the issues at stake and the probable outcome of them. They could have reached the pass before noon of the next day, since the little Dutchman had a good road, and for a long way it was clear of the hills. But Stagg held the horses to a steady, even pace, out of regard for the gunman's aching head, and the midday rays of the sun were baking the mountains when they came at last to the mouth of the deep natural cut in the hills which was Lobo Pass.

Kurt, who had dozed fitfully in the saddle, shook himself wide awake, and scrutinized the towering side walls of the pass intently. The vertical moss-seamed slabs glistened in the sun. There was nowhere anything that even remotely resembled the entrance to a cave.

Stagg rode steadily on till he was well into the main depth of the pass, and came abreast a cutback in the towering right-hand wall. The cutback, almost perfectly rectangular in form, was a good hundred yards deep and slightly over two hundred yards long. It was not an unusual formation in a territory where the hills were merely rearing escarpments of stone covered by a thin layer of earth. The high walls were so sheer that they overhung a little at the lip, nearly five hundred feet overhead. The floor of the cutback was always mostly in the shade.

At the lower centre of the cutback close to the

foot of the wall, there bubbled a never-failing spring, like a lone relic of the vanished river that once had carved the deep cut of Lobo Pass through the hills. There were always yards of grass and verdure growing along the spring and the creek that flowed from it, and in the shade of the cutback walls. Seven tall poplars shaded the spring, the suckers from their roots and bases banked in a hedge of brush. Four live oaks grew by the poplars.

As Stagg drew abreast of the poplar-shaded spring, he swerved the horses into the cutback. In the shadow of the towering wall beside the live oaks he halted the animals, dismounted, untied Quillan, and forced him to dismount also, retaining a hard grip on the outlaw's arm. He motioned with his other hand toward the wall behind the poplars and oaks.

"Now listen, Kurt. The entrance to the cave is back there. We're going in, and you're staying there till your jaw is well. I'm warning you that I'll be watching you. Don't try to escape. Better men than you have tried to get away from me. They didn't make it. I don't want to have to beat you up, but I'll break every bone in your carcass before I'll let you give me the slip. And don't think I can't do it. Have you got that?"

There was in the outlaw's face the same look as had been there when he confronted Stagg in the Idle Hour; that same aura of pent force quivering to be released. His full curved mouth curled in an insolent sneer.

"I've got it. I got it before you wasted a perfectly good breath saying it. And I warn you right now that you'll have to do some watching to keep me from getting away. I'll beat it the first chance."

"Try it, an you'll find it the sorriest thing you ever did. Come on. We're both hungry. I can manage to rig you up a pretty stout soup from the stuff I have in there."

Still gripping Kurt's arm, he guided him past the poplars to the wall, then along the wall beyond the oaks till they were both completely hidden from all possible observance behind the poplar growth. There he drew Kurt to a halt, and the outlaw looked up with puzzled scrutiny.

Nothing was here but the rearing wall, composed of ancient tiers of stone slabs, the chinks between the slabs grown thick with mosses and wild weeds.

Stagg reached up a hand and pushed upon one slab that looked quite like all the rest. It gave and swung, like a door on a pivot. The mosses and weeds on one edge remained undisturbed, growing solidly on the stone next the pivoting slab. The mosses and weeds on the other edge swung outward on the edge of the slab itself. The slab was a little over five feet in height, barely four feet in width. There showed at one side of it a narrow opening scarcely two feet wide, and yawning blackness beyond.

Stagg shoved Quillan through the narrow opening, then himself crowded through. The air within was cool and fresh, and once through the narrow portal Quillan found that he could stand upright. He wondered why the atmosphere was not dank and unpleasant.

"Just a minute," said Stagg. "I've a lantern right here."

He closed the slab behind them, leaving them in pitch darkness, took a match from his pocket and struck a light. A lantern hung upon a stout root end thrusting in at one edge of the slab. He lighted it, and there was revealed ahead a long narrow corridor vaulting away overhead to a height of eight to ten feet. The two men started down the corridor, the lantern's rays breaking the darkness as they advanced.

"Don't be afraid of stumbling," Stagg said quietly. "The floor's good all the way. We'll have daylight back here pretty quick, and we can do away with the lantern. There's a break in the outside wall. You can't locate it from the outside, and you can't reach it from the inside, but it lets in a lot of light. Here, you turn to the left. This is the cave."

One abrupt turn in the widening corridor, a right-angle advance of ten feet, and they walked out into the main cavern.

Here the vault of the roof swept steeply upward for sixty feet or more, lost in darkness at the top. The crevice in the outside wall, some twenty feet overhead, was a long, clean break lengthwise of the roof of the cavern, a great natural skylight, through which the sun's rays were pouring downward, offering perfect ventilation.

The lower interior of the cave was as light as any ordinary room in a house. It comprised one rock-walled room, roughly circular, varying from thirty to forty feet in diameter. It was Stagg's secret retreat, his palace of solitude.

It was furnished with two tables and several chairs Stagg had made of buckskin and hand-hewn poplar wood. There was a rocking-chair and two bunks made of the same materials. There were five black bearskin rugs on the stone floor, pelts of bears Stagg had killed, skins he had cured. There was a rock fireplace under one end of the crevice, rather a sort of rude rock stove. There was a rough cupboard beside it, shelves stocked with canned goods, dried venison, beef jerky, enamelled ware for food and some cooking utensils.

On one corner of a table were a large tin of tobacco and three pipes. Stagg turned weary eyes on the gunman.

"Make yourself at home. I'll get us something to eat, then I'll go out and tether the horses."

Quillan surveyed him curiously. "I suppose you did all this."

"Every stick of it."

"How did you find the cave?"

Stagg laughed. "I chased a rabbit into it. I shot him and he ducked in by the slab. I followed him. This has been my getting-away place ever since. I've been years fixing it up the way I wanted it."

Quillan's blue eyes turned cold and ugly. "You might as well spill it, Stagg. What the devil have you to do with me?"

Stagg's black eyes were unreadable. "You'll find out when I get ready for you to know. Don't ask questions. I'm not sure where I am myself, yet, Kurt. Sit down there where I can watch you. And you might write this down to remember: the first move you make to escape I'll fix you so you won't try it again. If you don't want to be tied hand and foot all the time you're here, behave yourself."

The outlaw made no answer. He sat down in the chair Stagg designated. He knew that when he did move to escape nothing would stop him, because he would not try it till he was certain his attempt would succeed.

He ate the soup and canned milk and coffee Stagg prepared and set before him. The meal over, Stagg calmly did tie him hand and foot and went out to tether the horses on good feeding ground for the rest of the day.

That night he tied Kurt to his bunk. For four days he watched and fed him, and tied him in his bunk at night. In the pocket of his shirt Stagg had one package of tailor-made cigarettes, a package about half full. Jay Stokes had given them to him. He shared them with Kurt. The second day in the cave Kurt managed to secrete one of them in his own shirt pocket, and that night he hid it, after dark, in a crevice in the wall below the top of the bunk.

For two days he watched and manœuvred before he managed to secure and secrete in the same place two matches. On the fourth day, in the late afternoon, Stagg got up to go change the horses' feeding ground. He tied Kurt in his bunk to secure him during his absence, as he had made a habit of doing.

Then he went out of the cavern, and down the long corridor that led to the outside. He was no more than out of sight when Kurt's fingers carefully worked the cigarette and matches out of the crevice. He got the cigarette lighted with the second match.

The rope which bound him was escape proof, unless he had some way of severing the rope. It ran underneath the bunk, looped and tied around each wrist, and was doubled back under the bunk, the ends tied there where the bound man could not possibly reach them by any process. The rope running from his wrists under and around the bunk was short enough that he could not bring his hands together, and his feet were tied in the same fashion by a separate rope. So that he was spread-eagled upon the bunk, with barely enough play of the rope to allow him decent comfort.

He had to bend his head far to one side to get the cigarette into his mouth. The first match broke in his fingers, but the second lighted, and the cigarette took fire from it. He flipped the match aside and bent his head still farther. The rope was a fine hard-woven cotton line. A man couldn't possibly break it by exerting pressure against it: not only was it too stout to be so broken, but it was fine enough to cut into a man's wrists and make the pain of the effort beyond endurance.

Kurt raised his right hand as far as it would come, and set the burning end of the cigarette against the rope just beyond his wrist. He had all he could do to achieve that position. His neck and arm muscles began to cramp almost immediately, but he held the cigarette there doggedly, blowing upon it, puffing only fre-quently enough to keep the coal alive.

His wired jaws didn't make the task any easier. The hard surface of the cotton rope did not take fire readily.

Two minutes passed, and the cigarette was half gone, before the first spark caught and glowed in the rope fibre. He blew upon it gently. The spark grew and ate steadily into the fibre, ever more rapidly, as fire eats into the punk sticks children use for lighting firecrackers. The rope began to give, and the outlaw held to the straining effort with grim persistence, though he was beginning to wonder if he could endure long enough.

Then the rope began to part. The creeping spark increased. The cigarette stub was now so short that he felt it painfully hot against his lips. He tugged furiously with his hand. The rope flew apart, both ends glowing and smoking. It had taken him five minutes.

He jerked the rope from under the bunk with his left hand, loosed the double knot, tore it from his left wrist and threw it to the floor. He removed the second rope from his feet and leaped off the bunk. He paused only long enough to grind under heel the smoking ends of the rope he had burned in two. Then he went out of the cavern and down the corridor at a run. Twice he stumbled in the dark, caught himself and plunged on.

He was certain Stagg had brought his guns to the cave, but he had no time to look for them. He must reach his horse and be gone before Stagg was aware of his escape.

By the time the outlaw had emerged warily from the cutback into the pass, Stagg had reached the gully where the horses were, he had been careful to elicit that information from Stagg and set it in his brain for future use. He reached the ridge, looking into the gully in time to see Stagg moving the horses and tethering them several yards beyond. He crouched in the cover of the trees, waiting tensely for Stagg to be gone.

The instant Stagg passed from sight on his way back to the cave, Quillan was slipping swiftly down the slope toward the horses. He had not dared burden himself with his heavy riding gear; he had dared chance nothing that could slow his speed in getting away from the cave. He had ridden bareback before. It was a small consideration.

Stagg crossed the cutback with his mind intent on getting the evening meal. He swung the slab aside, closed it and went up the corridor at a long stride. He knew it too well to need a light. But as he stepped inside the main cavern he had a feeling that his eyes were tricking him, that what he saw could not be as he saw it.

The bunk on which he had left Kurt Quillan was empty.

With a furious oath, Stagg dashed across the cavern. The cigarette stub and the burned and blackened ends of the rope, like two small smudges of soot upon the grey slabs of the floor, told him what had happened. He couldn't understand how Kurt had at any time managed to get hold of either cigarette or matches.

He whirled and went out of the corridor a great deal more quickly than he had come down it. He knew it was hopeless before he reached the gully, but he had to make sure.

His steps slowed and he felt his muscles tighten with his anger as he came within sight of the spot where the horses had been tethered. Both the Arabian and the big white Skater were gone. With neither saddle nor bridle, with only a rope to fashion a hackamore, the outlaw had ridden away, leaving Stagg afoot at Lobo Pass.

And Lobo Pass was twenty miles from the nearest ranch.—

That ranch was the Seven Up, lying between the pass and the Circle G. It was owned by burly, red-faced Pat Ryan. Stagg was as near to losing control of himself as he could ever remember being, but he turned right there, without even going back to the cave, and started toward the Seven Up. Let Kurt circle back to the cave if he cared to. His guns weren't there. No guns were there. Stagg had purposely left them all at the livery stable with Jay Stokes.

As Stagg walked down the pass toward the trail that would lead him to the Seven Up, Quillan was riding down Seco Trail to the north, leading the white gelding. By ten o'clock that night, the outlaw was approaching the north-west corner of the Circle G. He turned Skater loose to find his way home, and rode on.

He left Seco Trail behind and turned west into the open range.

CHAPTER VI

THE MAN FROM CHICAGO

AT nine o'clock the next morning, Doctor Mordan and Micky sat down to a late breakfast. They were still at the table, drinking a second cup of coffee when Bill Stagg rode up to the front walk on a Seven Up horse, and came toward the house with his dark face as ominous as a thunder-head.

Micky saw him through the window, and sat tense, waiting, as he came up on the porch, and Mordan heard his footsteps and went to open the door.

The doctor said nothing, after one look at Stagg's face. Stagg advanced into the dining-room and dropped into a chair. He was haggard with weariness.

"Kurt got away," he said, and there was more than bitterness in the rumble of his voice. He told them how the outlaw had managed the escape. "Yesterday afternoon, around five o'clock. I had to walk all the way to the Seven Up, damn him! Didn't get there till midnight. I borrowed a horse from Pat and I've been riding ever since. I'm tired. Could I have a cup of coffee, Micky?"

"Of course." The girl rose quickly. "And fried potatoes and bacon and eggs. There's plenty of potatoes left, and I can cook the bacon and eggs while you're drinking one cup of coffee."

She went hurriedly toward the kitchen, startled at the exultation that leaped up within her at the knowledge that Quillan had got away. She carried Stagg a cup of hot coffee, and asked whether Kurt had taken his guns, her eyes veiled from Stagg's penetrating scrutiny.

She was not sure whether she was relieved or uneasy to learn that Kurt was without a weapon. He had no way to defend himself, no agent of intimidation to prevent other men from shooting him down, and to ensure his escape. And there could be no doubt that any man on the Seco, seeing him free of Stagg, coming upon him there where the open range stretched, would shoot him down.

And Micky realized, as she bent over the kitchen stove, that in the hours he had been there, during which she had ministered to him, and talked to him, and even a time or two dreamed of him as she slept, he had ascended to a place of importance in her scheme of things. Any close contact with a man of his dynamic pent force could not end tamely and leave no impression.

He had come there a patient for the doctor; the bad man and killer of the Seco range. Before he had gone he had become to her Kurt Quillan, a being rare, and a sad memory indeed should he die as he had lived, a burning spirit shining with romance should he win free of the Seco and blaze his better trail.

She started into the dining-room, a cup of coffee for Stagg in her hands, aware that she was praying with all the will she had that no one would come into contact with Kurt before he was clear of the danger zone where his life was forfeit.

Stagg looked up at her as she set the cup of steaming coffee before him, then they both turned their heads in involuntary inquiry as a step sounded on the front porch. There was a knock on the door.

Mordan uncoiled his long lean frame and rose with a grunt of impatience. "Huh! People always getting sick or hurt at the most inopportune times, damn it! I wonder what now."

A stranger faced him when he opened the door, a man who did not belong to the range, who had come from some place far off. He was carrying a small bag in one hand.

The man was of medium height, very thin, of middle age or over, and his hair that once had been brown was cinnamon grey. His eyes were brown. He was dressed in an ordinary grey business suit. As he smiled a greeting at the doctor, the doctor saw that all of the man's upper teeth were crowned with gold. You didn't see that often, the doctor thought fleetingly. It marked a man. Then the stranger spoke.

"Good morning. Are you Doctor Mordan?"

"I am. What can I do for you?"

"My name is Barnes, doctor—Owen Barnes. I am looking for a man named Alonzo Ivey. The agent at the railway station said you could tell me where to find him. He said you knew everybody."

Mordan's thin face lighted with a humorous smile. "Yes, a doctor does get around. But it's a long way to Lon Ivey's place. You'd better come in and have a bite to eat with us. We've just been having late breakfast. You'd be welcome."

Barnes shook his head. "Thanks, doctor; but I ate on the train. I'd rather go right on, if you'll kindly direct me. I'm in something of a hurry to reach the Ivey place."

"Well, it's not hard to find." Mordan stepped out onto the porch. "You go about sixty miles southwest to Seco Springs, by the road. That's the road about a hundred yards down yonder, branching off this street. Just stay on the main road, and you can't get off. It doesn't go any place but to Seco Springs. When you get into Seco Springs, go into the Idle Hour Saloon and ask Swabs to direct you to Lon Ivey's ranch. You might forget if I gave you the directions all the way now. You can get a pretty good lunch at the Idle Hour, too, by the way."

"Any stage running to Seco Springs?"

The doctor stared a little. He glanced down at the name tag on Barnes's hand bag. "I thought you must be from the city, all right. No, there's no stage up here, Mr. Barnes! The only way for you to get there is to wait till somebody is driving that way with team and wagon; anybody would be glad to give you a lift. Or you can rent a saddle horse. Do you ride?"

"If I can get a well-behaved horse, doctor."

"That solves it, then. See that big white house across the street? Jay Stokes's place. He owns the livery stable. He can rent you a good horse. I'm sure you won't have any trouble finding Lon."

"No, I don't believe I will. Thank you."

Barnes turned away and went briskly down the walk, and the doctor returned slowly to the dining-room, a frown on his lean face, his grey brows drawn almost together in a scowl.

"Seems to me a lot of queer things are happening lately," he said as he slipped into a chair across the table from Stagg, and Micky looked at him in surprise.

"Queer—for a man to ask directions to somebody's ranch?"

"This is a cow town, Micky," the doctor answered. "Most of the people that pass through on the railroad just pass through, and that's all. You never see any one around here but the ranchers, the cowboys, a few buyers in season, and traders now and then. Business men from the East just don't come in here asking to be directed to somebody's ranch. They just don't do it! Isn't that right, Bill?"

"Yes, I'm afraid it is, doc. Far as I know, it never did happen before."

Mordan's shrewd grey eyes narrowed. "Oh, yes it did, Bill. That's what's queer about it. It happened about two months ago. A big tall fellow about Kurt's size got off the train, came over here and asked me to tell him the way to Lon Ivey's ranch."

Micky had returned to the kitchen to hurry along the rest of Stagg's breakfast, but she worked noiselessly, walking on tiptoe, listening to what her uncle was telling.

She heard Stagg's deep bass:

"He did, eh? Well, that is something out of the ordinary, doc. What did he want of Lon?"

"I couldn't say. Listen, Bill; there's something queer going on, and the thought just struck me that it might be coming closer home than I'd imagined, I'll explain as briefly as I can, and see what you think. The fellow that came here two months ago said his name was Warren Cottrelle, and that he was from Chicago. I gave him the same directions I gave this man Barnes just now. He rented that big red-and-white pinto from Jay Stokes, and started for Ivey's place. He passed through Seco Springs and asked directions of Swabs, as I'd told him to do. Then he faded right out into thin air."

Micky came into the room with fried potatoes, eggs, and bacon. "Uncle Dan! Are you insinuating that he never reached the Ivey place?"

"He never did. About two weeks later the pinto came roaming in by itself, with all the gear still on it. The horse wasn't saddle galled and it had been eating regular, so it would seem that it hadn't been wearing the gear all that time. There was a note tied in its mane. The note said, 'Sorry to have kept your horse so long. Many thanks.' It was signed Warren G. Cottrelle. But—about a month later I saw Lon out on the open range, and he said Cottrelle never came there, he didn't know who Cottrelle was, he had never even heard of him and couldn't imagine what he wanted of him."

Stagg's black eyes rested, hard and intent, on the doctor's thin features. "Anybody else know about this, doc?"

"Only Swabs and Pete Gulick. I told Swabs to keep his mouth shut about it. I told Pete about Cottrelle to see what he thought, and to find out if he'd seen anything of the fellow. He hadn't, and he didn't know what to make of it. And here's the second one coming looking for Ivey —so he says! I don't like it, Bill."

"I don't like anything about it!" said Stagg.

"And this Barnes is from Chicago, too," the doctor went on. "I saw it on his bag name tag."

"Do you think something happened to this

Cottrelle?" asked Micky. "Do you think somebody did away with him?"

"Well, Kurt was somewhere up there loose in the hills when Cottrelle disappeared," answered Mordan bluntly. "But I don't really think anything like that happened. There was that note tied in the pinto's mane, remember, though anybody could have written it. How would Jay Stokes know what Cottrelle's handwriting looked like?

"I'll tell you what I do think. I have an idea this Cottrelle wasn't looking for Lon Ivey at all: I think that was just a stall, to give him an excuse to go poking around in that part of the country without rousing too much curiosity. He was looking for somebody, all right. But—it wasn't Lon Ivey."

"Then who was it?" Stagg's voice was hard, tight.

"That's as far as I got, Bill. But I'd be willing to bet a lot that I'm right. Asking for Lon was a blind. They both of them have some shady business on this range, and they simply got the name of some rancher in this territory and used it for their stall; it wouldn't matter whose name it was, so long as it wasn't the man they really were looking for."

"But how would they get the name of a Seco rancher away back there in Chicago?" protested Micky.

"Stockyards," said Stagg. "Beef herds from the

95

Seco, Micky; when they're weighed in there are records, receipts, waybills. Anybody could go down to the stockyards and get the name of a rancher on this range."

"Oh, I see. But what can they be doing out here, Uncle Dan?"

"That's another thing I can't figure yet, Micky. Lon Ivey says Lispy Louie acted damned peculiar for several days after Cottrelle disappeared —and anybody going to the L I to see Lon would have to pass Lispy Louie's Crazy L first."

"Well," said Stagg slowly, "maybe these two men were in reality looking for Louie, doc."

The doctor's grey eyes flicked quickly to Stagg's expressionless face. "That would seem the obvious conclusion, wouldn't it? Lispy Louie is just the kind of fellow who might be mixed up in some shady deal. But I wouldn't try to get any information out of anybody as slippery as Louie. I'd be licked before I started. He's like an eel."

Stagg suddenly laid down his fork, his black eyes stilled by a sudden arresting thought. "Didn't you say it was about two months ago that this Cottrelle came here?"

"Just about, Bill. What's struck you?"

"By gad, doc, you're right! Something screwy is going on, something that needs a little looking into; and I'm going to appoint myself a committee of one to do the looking. You and I know that there's never been any cattle stealing on the

Seco range, we've never had the least trouble that way. But about six weeks ago, Lon Ivey dropped into the Idle Hour; one of our boys was there and he told me about it. Lon said that Lispy Louie had been stealing some of his young stuff and changing the brands on them. And he said that if Louie didn't cut it out, he'd stop it for him. He said there'd never been any cow stealing going on around here, and he wasn't going to see it started on his place. There's a tie-up there, doc. Where was it Lispy saw Kurt? Up there at the north-east edge of the L I. There's a tie-up there, too. Too many queer things coming to light in the same spot not to be tied up. And if Kurt's mixed up in anything like that, I'm going to know just how deep he has got himself into a mess."

"Listen here, Bill." The doctor leaned on the table, and his grey eyes fixed on Stagg as if they would look through him. "I've always liked you. All of us that know you think you're one of the best of us, and we wouldn't want to see anything happen to you. Why do you want to go messing into what might turn out to be a pretty nasty piece of business, just because Kurt Quillan may be mixed up in it? Here you've lived right up there on the Circle G for years, and kept so much to yourself that you never even come into contact with Kurt till now. And you yourself deliberately bring that about. What can that young hellion mean to you, Bill?"

Stagg drew a hard harsh breath, and a veil clouded all expression from his black eyes. His face set like a mask.

"Doc, I guess I'd better explain. I can't explain very much, because I don't know the answers myself. I can only tell you why I have to stick to Kurt till he's in the clear or under the dirt. A lot of years ago, doc, I loved a woman. I think she loved me, too; I know she did. But she was married to another man, and he was a good fellow, and she had no complaint against him. We just loved each other, and we couldn't help that, but I wouldn't be to blame for breaking up another man's home.

"I just quietly went away. A few years later I heard that her husband had died, and I went back to the town where she lived, as fast as I could get there, only to find that she was gone. I followed her. But I caught up with her too late. Her name was Bess Quillan."

The doctor caught his breath on an astounded cry. "Bill!"

"Yes. That's it." Stagg's eyes were bleak with an old pain. "I followed her all the way to Lobo Pass. I found her in Lobo Pass. Dead. I was just coming into the pass when I heard gunfire, and I forced my horse into a run. It was at that time of evening when the dusk is thick, but it isn't really dark yet. The man who had killed Bess heard me coming, took a shot at me, and rode off the other way. One glance was enough to tell me Bess was dead, and Kurt, he was three years old then, was crouched there by her body crying his eyes out.

"I raced on after the killer. I emptied my gun at him. I thought by the way he swayed once in the saddle that I'd hit him along the right arm or shoulder. I couldn't be sure. He got clean away. I turned back into the pass to get Kurt and pick up Bess. But some other passer-by, attracted by the sound of firing, was there before me. He had Kurt in his arms, and Kurt was still crying, but the fellow was wiping tears from his own eyes, and patting Kurt on the shoulder. He looked honest and kind. I was a stranger, and I was wearing a gun that was still hot from being recently emptied. You can see where that would have put me.

"I faded. But I stayed close enough to watch. I saw the rancher finally get Kurt quieted. Bess's horse had got frightened away, and the night was coming on fast. The rancher tied Bess's body into the saddle, and started out of the pass leading the horse and carrying Kurt. And, by gad, he carried him all the way to the Seven Up, till he could get another horse. I followed him all the way to his own ranch. That was Lem Strickland. I stuck around to see what he was going to do. When he buried Bess and let it be known that he was going to keep Kurt and raise him, I was satisfied.

"He could do a lot better by Kurt than I could. But I took a kind of vow to myself that I'd stay close and watch over Bess's boy. I holed away in a hideout I'd found up in the pass for a while. Then I got a job with Pete Gulick, and I've been there ever since, watching Kurt grow up, but keeping to my own affairs. For the last year I've been pretty sick over the way he was going, but I didn't know what I could do about it. I held my hand and my tongue, and sat on pins from month to month, hoping he'd snap out of it, and maybe light out for some other place, and do better. But when the posse started out to hunt him down and string him up, I—damn it, I couldn't stand seeing that happen to Bess's boy, so I went after him myself.

"So now you know all I know. I'm going up there and do a little looking around the L. I and the Crazy L. If I can make sure that Kurt isn't mixed up with whatever's going on there, I'll come back and let them settle their own mess. But if I do find that Kurt's concerned with it, I'll rip it wide open. There's some reason for that boy suddenly going on the loose about a year ago. He wasn't born bad. He had a good father and a good mother, and Lem and Mrs. Strickland gave him a good home.

"There's something awfully wrong about the whole business, and I'm going to get at the bottom of it before it's too late, if there's any way of doing it. That's all, doc."

"Just a minute, Bill. Lem was alive when you found him. He'd only been dead about an hour when I got there to the L-Over-S. He had to be alive when you found him. But—did he talk? Did he say anything worth repeating?"

"He didn't talk much, doc. He was too near gone. He did say that Kurt shot him. He said Kurt and some other fellow were shooting at each other from cover, and he tried to stop Kurt, and Kurt shot him."

"Who was the other fellow?"

"Lem didn't know, doc. He was under cover, and he ducked when Lem barged into the fight. That was about all Lem said, before he passed clear out. I know what you're thinking. I wanted to know who the other fellow was, too. I asked Kurt several times while I had him there in the cave, and he wouldn't tell me. Listen! There goes our friend Barnes. I have an idea."

The sound of a horse's hoofs walking over a board platform came from across the street, and the three in the doctor's dining-room rose to go into the front room and look out the window.

The man Barnes was riding across Stokes's wooden sidewalk, astride the big red-and-white pinto that Cottrelle had rented two months before. Stagg turned from the window with a grim smile.

"Yes, I'm going to look into it, doc. I'll rent myself a fresh horse from Jay Stokes, and I'll be back as soon as I can learn anything that's worth while knowing."

"Barnes is on the way," said Mordan, "but I'll

make you a bet, Bill. I'll bet you that he never gets to the L I. Want to take me up on that?"

"I don't think I'd better, doc. You just might lose. And listen, doc. Do something for me." The huge man's smooth dark face was no mask now. Pain, and regret, and something that might have been a flicker of vague wild hope, made mobile his features and glittered in his black eyes. "If somebody don't shoot Kurt, he's going to come back here to have those wires taken off in a few days. Can't you sock him full of hop, or something, and tie him up and keep him here? I know you don't like the idea of having him around, on account of Micky, but I—"

"I guess things have changed a little, Bill." Mordan interrupted. "Micky did something to him. We all know it, now. We really knew it that night when you took him away, Micky, and I— too late. You needn't worry. If I get him in my hands again, he'll stay here. And I'll leave him to Micky and keep my hands behind me and my damned mouth shut."

Stagg turned slowly to the girl, who had been listening in silence ever since he had first spoken of Bess Quillan. She raised her amber eyes to his, and he saw that they were bright and shining, as if they had recently been wet. The smile on her face was wry and thin.

"I know better now, Bill, why I felt about him as I did. You're right, Bill; you're right!

Something happened to turn that man into a killer. He didn't do it just because he wanted to. Get up there as fast as you can. You can save a man's soul sometimes when you can't save his life. If ever he gets here, Bill—I'll be waiting for him."

CHAPTER VII

WHO WAS THE OTHER MAN?

BILL STAGG went across to Stokes's barn, secured a fresh horse, left the Seven Up horse there to rest and feed, and took the road for Seco Springs, a short half hour after Owen Barnes had departed in the same direction.

Due north of Arroyo, a few miles west of the Seco Trail, Kurt Quillan roused from a long sleep under heavy overhanging branches, untied the Arabian from the tree where he had tethered him, looped the rope hackamore over his nose, and started due west, toward the Crazy L. He rounded a clump of brush, and came face to face with a mounted horseman, who patently had heard the Arabian's hoofbeats and had paused there to see what rider was coming.

Without a chance at self-defence, Kurt was run head-on into what amounted to a trap.

The man on the other horse was Lon Ivey. Ivey was a smaller man than Quillan, a man with a square, sun-tanned face, shaved smooth, his hair and brows black above mild-looking hazel eyes. The eyes were anything but mild the instant they recognized Kurt Quillan.

Quillan's cold eyes stilled as they saw Ivey reach for his gun. He had one hope of escape from certain death. His heels were more swift than Ivey's hand. Kurt rolled his rowels to the flanks of a horse that did not know the jab of a spur. The Arabian reared wildly, and plunged ahead in a high, clean leap, straight at Ivey. The movement was a surprise manœuvre, but it wasn't quite quick enough. Ivey's gun crashed from the open end of his holster, and he drove spurs to his own mount to get out of the Arabian's way.

Kurt felt the thud of Ivey's bullet tear into his side below the right shoulder. From somewhere close, to the north, a wild shout raised. With a loud and angry curse, Ivey wheeled his horse and crashed through the brush to the west.

Kurt pulled the Arabian around and started toward the south, away from the vicinity of that shout which had come from so close to the north. Before he had gone a hundred yards his blue shirt was soggy with the blood from the wound in his side, and he was so sick and dizzy he couldn't keep his seat on the horse's back any longer. He swayed, and the landscape began to stagger drunkenly before his eyes. He dragged on the rope, and brought the Arabian to a halt, striving to get off the horse before he fell off. He literally lurched to the ground, half spun about on his heel, and fell sprawling, senseless before he hit the earth.

He did not hear the drum of another horse's hoofs, approaching from the north, draw close, dash past him and race on in pursuit of Ivey. This horse was a flea-bitten grey, and the man on its back was a small man, in a faded-blue, patched shirt, a stained low-crowned tan hat, and ragged red angora chaps.

The scrawny grey couldn't overtake any horse on that range, but the little man in the red angora chaps pounded its ribs with his heels, and the horse did its panting best. Then Ivey came again into sight in an open spot, and the man on the flea-bitten grey got one good look at his face. The man in the red chaps turned about and rode back to where Kurt Quillan lay, pulled his horse to a halt, flung himself off and knelt by Kurt. He drew Kurt's blood-soaked shirt from under his belt and examined the wound. The heavy bullet had torn the flesh badly and raked a rib. Small splinters of bone were thrusting up through the flesh.

The little man in the red chaps stood up and looked around. There was no water nearer than a couple of miles. He decided to try to get Kurt onto the Arabian and get him to the creek, but when he tried to lift Kurt's body, the outlaw opened his eyes, returning to consciousness. He looked up with a pained grimace, and saw the red chaps, the faded-blue shirt, and under the tan stained hat the dark face of Lispy Louie le Grande.

Louie, seeing that Kurt was conscious again, let him gently down to the ground.

"It was Lon Ivey, damn him!" said Kurt thickly.

"Yeah, I know. I thaw him," replied Louie. "What are you doing out here? I thought Bill Thtagg had you holed up thomewhere. Whereth your gunth?"

Kurt's gaze fixed on Louie's face in that still cold stare, his senses fully cleared now. "I got away from Stagg. He hid my guns somewhere."

"Well, if you can manage to ride, I'll help you get onto your horthe." Louie's cocked eye swung aside, to let the other eye rest in some anxiety on the outlaw's drawn features. "I'll let you have my thaddle and bridle, and I'll ride bareback. You think you can hang on long enough to get in to Doc Mordan?"

Kurt braced himself and sat up, weaving a little, dizzily, and the cold-blue eyes seemed chill enough to have frozen Louie's dark greasy skin. "Just what am I to make of you, Louie? You do your damnedest to shoot me full of lead from ambush, and now you want to help me to the doctor when somebody else puts a slug in me."

"Me? Thootin' at you from ambush?" The

astonishment on the greasy face was unmistakably real. Perspiration started on Louie's forehead and mingled with the exudation of natural oil. The cocked eye rolled wildly. "I never thot at you from any plathe! I've thot at a few jathperth, and pinked a few, though I never killed none that I know of. But tho help me, I never took a thot at you. Why, what would I want to thoot at you for?"

Kurt picked up his fallen blue beaver hat, and began to fan his face with it, gripping himself with grim control against the dizzy wave that assaulted his brain. "Louie, I have to get to Doctor Mordan and I know it. Up until the last few days I haven't cared whether I lived or not. But I'm taking a hand in a new game, and I'm going to live and take the winning tricks if God will let me. Only, before I start for Arroyo, I want to ask you a couple of questions. Are you telling me, on your word of honour, that it wasn't you who started shooting at me from the brush the morning Lem Strickland was killed?"

"If you can take my word of honour and believe it," answered Louie bitterly. "It'th more'n thome would do. Yeth! That'th what I'm tellin' you! How could I be out there thootin' at you that mornin' when I wath home on my own ranch, and I can prove it! One of Pete Gulick'th men wath there after thome thrayth. The thrayth wath on my land, and I helped him round 'em up. It took uth all mornin' and he et dinner with me before he drove 'em on home! It wath Jerry Hulan, and you can athk him!"

"I don't need to ask him." Fire began to cloud the clean cold-blue eyes. "I know when a man's telling the truth. You aren't that good at pretending, Louie. But then, who the devil was there that day, wearing a stained old tan hat like yours, and a faded-blue shirt like yours, and old red chaps like yours, with a red bandanna tied over his face?"

"You can thearch me!" Louie's bitterness rose. "And you can thearch me why he'd want to make you think it wath me, too. I don't know. But—thay! Ith that why you wath up by my plathe lookin' around the day I theen you and went and told Bill Thtagg?"

"That's it, Louie. I was certainly looking for you. You'll never know how close you came to getting yourself filled with lead when you rode up there and gave me Bill's message. What made you go and tell Stagg you saw me there? You weren't afraid of me, and both of us know it."

"Well, I—I—" Louie floundered, and the cocked eye rolled again, and he wiped the sweat from his face with an old green bandanna he took from his pocket. "I knew the pothee would get you if thomebody didn't do thomething, and I didn't want 'em to, and the only perthon that I could trutht to do anything for me wath Bill

108

Thtagg. Tho I went and athked him if he wouldn't do thomethin' to keep you from gettin' thtrung up before it wath too late. That'th all."

"Oh, so that's all! Why any such concern for me, Louie? What could it matter to you how soon somebody flattened me out in the dirt? Quick, Louie! What's back of this?"

Another motion distorted the greasy features of Lispy Louie. "I won't tell! I jutht know that thomebody'th tryin' to cheat you out of thomethin' that belongth to you. And I'm not guethin', either! I know! And that ain't fair. And bethidth, I hate the man that'th tryin' to cheat you. He tried to do me dirt."

The outlaw sat motionless. His head had cleared, but his side was beginning to hurt and burn, though it had almost ceased to bleed. He turned his cold, quiet gaze upon Louie's sweating, fear-drawn face. "Listen, Louie. You're making several wild statements that can't possibly be true. You're making an insane error, some way. I never owned anything in my life to be cheated out of but my Arabian horse. What makes you think I did?"

"How old are you?" asked Louie bluntly.

"I'll be twenty-one on my next birthday, which is exactly two weeks from to-morrow. Why?"

"How do you know?"

"Why, my mother had a sort of little record book in which she had written down a lot of things about me, and she had pasted some little pictures of me in it. Lem found it among her things when he finally caught her horse, and he saved it for me."

"Well," said Louie grimly, "you manage to live till you're twenty-one, and you'll own one of the finetht rancheth on thith range, and a thwell houthe, and about ten thouthand head of prime cattle, and nothin' can thtop you from claimin' it but a bullet! And I ain't makin' no wild thtatementh and I ain't makin' no inthane error! I know what I'm talkin' about. And that fella that'th got your ranch ith thcared. He'll kill you off if he can. He'th been thootin' at you, he wath the one that wath thootin' at you when you killed Lem, and I'd bet on it. It jutht come to me, that it wath him."

"Who is it, Louie?" Quillan demanded tensely. "Who is it?"

Some of the fear went out of Lispy Louie; he seemed to grow suddenly sure of himself, almost coldly calculating, and his one good eye held steady on the outlaw's face.

"I ain't goin' to tell you who he ith. If I did, you'd go rippin' thingth open and thpoilin' every chance we got of gettin' thith thing cleaned up. You thee here, Kurt: you're a killer, that'th the name you got. Any man on thith range would thoot you on thight. All right. Where would you get off if you tryin' to clean thith

110

meth up by yourthelf? You'd get thix feet of dirt and a pine box, that'th what! Thomebody'd get you thure! Ain't that true?"

"Yes. Yes, I'm afraid it is, Louie." Kurt's hand raised to push back the chestnut hair clinging to his damp forehead. There was about him again the straining impotent passion of a man reborn blindly seeking any passage from the darkness into the light. "But—if you'd tell who this man is, and give some man a chance. Give Bill Stagg a chance at him."

"I'm goin' to give Bill a chanthe at him. But you let me talk for a minute. I know that hith ranch ith yourth: I've got the proof of that, and I've got it hid away where nobody but me'll ever find it. And that'th all I have got proof of! We go tryin' to tear thingth open now, and we'll looth on every count. I know in my own mind that the fellow whooth got your ranch ith doin' everything he can to get rid of you, and he'th thcared becauthe he knowth thomebody got that proof from him, and from where he'd been keepin' it thinth you wath a baby, and he'th afraid you'll get thight of it thomeway.

"It proveth that you own that ranch—but he had to keep it becauthe it altho proveth that if you'd die he ownth the ranch himthelf. He'll do anything to get rid of you. I don't know how many thingth he'th done already, but I ain't got a thread of proof againtht him. And we've got to

111

have that before we can make a move. The minute we can get him in a corner, I'll dig up that proof of ownerthip and thow it, but there ain't no uthe till we've got him cold.

"And that'th it, and that'th all of it. And he ain't goin' to be eathy to catch, either. He'th thlick enough to make you believe he'th your betht friend, then thoot you in the back, when you ain't lookin'.

"And I'm tellin' you all thith tho you'll have then the enough to go to Doc Mordan'th houthe and lay low till thomebody elthe can run thith jathper down. Bill Thtagg ith goin' to come to the doc'th plathe thure, lookin' for you. You tell him to come to my ranch ath quick ath he can get there. You come on now, and I'll help you onto your horthe, and we'll get goin'."

Leaning on little Louie, Kurt got to his feet, fighting another wave of dizziness caused by the effort, but able to reach the Arabian, still gripping Louie's arm to steady himself. Louie insisted on transferring his own saddle and bridle to Kurt's horse, and when it was done he helped Kurt into the saddle. Kurt looked down at him with a smile.

"Louie, you've got your points. How did you happen to come along in the nick of time and scare Lon off before he could do his duty to the world and fill me full of lead?"

"I didn't jutht happen along. I wath following

him. One of hith boyth thaid he wath going to thee Pete Gulick, and I wanted to find out what he and Pete wath up to. I don't like that little fat Dutchman, and he don't like me. But he and Lon can both go to hell right now. I'm goin' to get you to Doc Mordan. We'll get there about dark, and we'll keep under cover all the way. We'll get you there all right. You thure you can hang on?"

"Yes, I can make it all right, Louie. Get your nag and come along."

The ride was slow, and they took it easy, stopped at a couple of creeks where Kurt might drink and rest, and kept to cover discreetly all the way. But they had only some thirty milcs to go, and the dusk had barely fallen when they came within sight of the little town.

Micky opened the door to Louie's rap, and held the lamp high to see who was there, and she started back, paling at sight of Quillan, white and dizzy, the side of his blue shirt black with blood, holding himself steady by one arm around the shoulders of the greasy-faced little man who stood beside him. Kurt's eyes were closed, and he was barely able to keep on his feet.

"Kurt!" She was conscious of a swift stab of pain, of the sick sink of her heart. "Oh, Uncle Dan! Uncle Dan! Quick! Kurt's here, hurt." Her gaze swung to Lispy Louie. "Can you get him inside? Here, wait till I set the lamp down. I'll take his other arm."

"That'th all right. I can manage. He'th thtill pretty good at helpin' himthelf."

She heard the heavy lisp, subconsciously, and knew who he was, but that was all in the back of her mind, and nothing was to the fore but the importance of getting Quillan to a bed and ascertaining the extent of his injury. By the time she set the lamp down on the table, Louie had helped Kurt into the room and kicked the door shut, and Mordan had come from the adjoining room in answer to his niece's startled cry.

"Who did it?" Mordan demanded sharply, and his doctor concern for the injured overrode every other consideration, as his grey eyes flashed from his niece, now at Kurt's other side, to Kurt himself, and to Louie.

"Lon Ivey shot him," answered Louie. "Where'll we put him?"

"Right in here, Louie," Mordan answered, picking up a lamp and leading the way into the bedroom. "You and Micky get him down there on the bed and I'll see to him right away. Are you conscious, Kurt? Can you manage to speak?"

Kurt drew a deep sigh, as he relaxed on the bed, and the blue eyes opened, to look into the doctor's face. "Yes. I'm conscious—only just about played out." His gaze went on to Micky, and light grew in his eyes. "I'm all right—now." It was a light that even Lispy Louie could not mistake, and he remembered that Kurt had said

114

he was sitting in on a new game, and he understood.

The doctor drew aside the blood-stiffened shirt, made a quick examination, and stood erect. "Oh, that isn't so bad! It's laccerated a good deal, and the rib is splintered. But the bullet didn't lodge, and the rib isn't even broken. I'll have him fixed up in no time."

Micky half choked over a sob, and fought it back furiously. Kurt's gaze shot to her face, suddenly ablaze. She blinked back stinging tears, and tried to smile. "I was afraid—afraid that—"

"Shush!" said Mordan loudly. "He's lost a lot of blood, and it weakened him. And the poor devil hasn't had anything but soup and such damned stuff for a week, and I don't dare take those wires off for a few days yet, either. But I'll bet you can figure a lot of ways to concoct things to get down him and make him strong again."

"Wireth!" said Lispy Louie. And Micky nodded, and the doctor explained, and Louie added: "Ith that what maketh him talk tho funny? I wath wondering. Well, all I thtopped for wath to thee how bad he wath hurt. If he'th goin' to be all right, I'll be gettin' along. Could I pleathe talk to you, mith?"

Micky hesitated for an instant, and glanced at Kurt, over whom the doctor was already at work, and followed Louie into the kitchen. There the little man stopped and faced her.

"I gueth you know who I am. Everybody doeth when they hear me talk."

"Yes, I knew, Louie. I'm the doctor's niece. What did you want? Something about Kurt?"

"No, ma'am. About Bill Thtagg. Hath he been here?"

"He was here this morning, Louie. He's on his way to your ranch now. He was going first to Seco Springs."

"Oh. Well, that wath all I wanted—for him to come up there. I got to thee him. But if he'th gone to Theco Thpringth I can cut acroth country and get to the Crazy L before he doeth. Don't you let Kurt go anywhere, ma'am. If you do, thomebody'll kill him thure."

"He'll not go anywhere for a while, Louie!" Micky's delicate face was almost grim. "You may depend on that."

"That'th thwell. Well, I got to be goin'. G'by."

As he went out of the house, Micky was already hurrying through the doorway into the room where Kurt lay. She held gauze and scissors and probe, and watched in silence while the doctor worked, and Kurt lay with closed eyes waiting patiently till it was done, and the side was band-aged, and the blood-stiffened shirt removed. Mordan sent Micky out with the tray of waste and instruments, and while she was absent from the room, he undressed Kurt, put one of his own nightshirts on him, and got him under the covers.

116

When Micky returned, the doctor was hanging Kurt's trousers in the clothes closet, and Kurt lay drained and weary, but eased and at rest.

She went up and stood by the bed. His eyes had been open when she entered the room, searching for her, waiting, and the light grew in them again as she came to stand beside him. The doctor looked at his niece and the outlaw, and shook his head, and turned and walked out of the room.

In the cave, on the third day, Stagg had removed the bandage from the jaw, as Mordan had told him he could do. The swelling had quite subsided, the discolouration gone, and for the first time Micky saw Quillan's chiselled face unmarred. She hadn't known that he was quite so spectacularly good-looking. Being the kind of person who loved beauty for its own sake, for a little space all she saw was the mould of his features. Then he lifted a hand, groping toward her, and she took it, and almost wilted into the chair beside the bed.

"Oh, Kurt—Kurt! You almost frightened the life out of me. I'm positively weak."

"Thanks." The voice was weary, but something sang in it. "I don't deserve that. I wasn't looking for it. I wonder—I'm beginning to wonder, if there's the least chance for me. Can you pay in instalments, do you suppose?"

"I don't know—what you mean, Kurt."

"I mean—I mean I've killed eight men. If I could take a bullet for everyone, if I could win a new start, do you think maybe I could square the score some way like that? Do you suppose I'm in so deep I'll have to die to square it?"

"Don't! Nobody knows. Only God. You mustn't talk any more now. Rest, and get strong again. I'll get you something to build back that blood you lost, to start building it. After you rest a while you can talk all you want to."

"What can I have to eat, Micky? I'm so infernally sick of soup and canned milk. And I can't get much between my teeth."

"I know, but you'd be surprised what I can do. Tom and Jerry, with plenty of good whisky in it, and all the raw egg is strengthening. And boiled egg yolk mashed in milk, and even potatoes beaten into milk, and beef tea. Oh, I'll have you on your feet before you know it. I'm going to fix you something right now. You close your eyes and rest till I come back."

CHAPTER VIII

PUZZLE FOR LISPY LOUIE

OWEN BARNES had left Arroyo around ten o'clock that morning. Shortly after five o'clock that afternoon he reached Seco Springs, left the red-and-white pinto at the hitching rack and went into the Idle Hour, to find Swabs drinking a glass of whisky with Pete Gulick.

Swabs looked up as Barnes halted before the bar. "What'll you have, stranger?"

"Oh, I'll take the same," Barnes answered. "And if you can make me up a few sandwiches of some kind to take along, I'll have those, too. And can you direct me to the ranch owned by Lon Ivey?"

From under surprised brows, Swabs shot a covert glance at Pete Gulick as he turned for bottle and glass. He answered Barnes's question as he set the drink before him. "Yeah. Sure. Just keep going on this road till you come to the first forks. There you turn to the left. When you come to the second forks, turn to the right and keep going. The first ranch you pass is the Crazy L. The next one is the L I. You can't miss it. You a friend of Lon's?"

"A friend?" Barnes smiled as he lifted the glass. "I would hardly say that. I scarcely know the man. I simply want to see him on business."

He said nothing more. He waited till Swabs made up four sandwiches, paid for them and the drink and walked out, and went off up the road to the north on Stokes's red-and-white pinto.

As the man passed from sight, Swabs looked at the little fat Dutchman and exploded with an astonished oath. "Well, I'll be hung for a horse thief. Another one!"

"Yah. Anudder von." Gulick's round fat face was quivering with excitement. "Und riding Jay

Shtokes's red-und-white pinto, already! I got a notion to jump on my nag und follow dot feller. Too many damn queer things is going on around here yet!"

"What you want to follow him for?" demanded Swabs. "Don't be so damn curious, Pete. Curiosity gets people into trouble. Haven't you learned that yet? If he never gets to the L I, that's his hard luck. What did Bill Stagg do with Kurt Quillan?"

The little Dutchman relaxed against the bar with a worried frown. "Vell, dot's what I come in here to tell you already, only dot feller lookin' for de L I come in, and I don't get a chance to say it yet. I don't know where Bill took him, but Kurt got away from him. He was running loose mit himself on de open range, only dis morning. Lon was come over to see me, und he run smack dab into him, und he took von shot at him, und den he sees dot Kurt don't got a gun, und he couldn't shoot a man what ain't got noddings to defend himself, so he rides away."

"He didn't get him, eh?"

"Nein. He just knocked him out a liddle. Lon was sure of dot, because he circles back to take a look, und Lispy Louie comes along und picks Kurt up and takes him off to Arroyo. Must haf gone off to Doc Mordan, already. Und Lon comes to see me, und told me. He was thinking we better get up anudder posse and stop Kurt's foolishness, but I tell him we vait till we get a liddle bedder line on things. So I come over to ask you if maybe you got any word from Bill Stagg yet."

"Never seen a hair of him," said Swabs. "You want to leave some message in case he comes in?"

"Yah. You tell him I want to see him, und I don't mean maybe! I want to see him right away. Don't say noddings to nobody else. Don't tell nobody Kurt gets loose again. Maybe he don't get loose. Maybe Stagg lets him go already. Ve don't do noddings till I see Bill Stagg again. Well, I got to be jogging along. Don't take some wooden nickels, Swabs." He hitched up his chaps belt, which was always sliding down from his fat little belly, and walked out of the Idle Hour with a parting wave of the hand for Swabs.

He got his horse from the hitching rack, and rounded the corner of the saloon, to come face to face with Bill Stagg, who was waiting there for him. Stagg stepped close to Gulick's horse, and spoke before the little Dutchman could voice the astonishment that blanked his round fat face.

"Pete, if you see anything of Kurt Quillan, don't go taking a shot at him. He got away from me, and I haven't been able to get any line on him yet."

"Yah! So! I was thinking somedings was wrong. Your white nag come home by himself, without no saddle. But I don't tell nobody yet.

Und Kurt ain't running around loose mit himself no more, I bet you." And he told Stagg what he had related to Swabs.

Stagg's black eyes deepened, and his rumbling bass voice quickened. "Lon shot him! Well, unless he's pretty damn bad, Doc Mordan will pull him out of it. And doc will keep him there, so he's safe for a while. I might as well tell you now, Pete. I'm quitting the Circle G."

If Stagg had walked up and slapped his face, the little Dutchman couldn't have been more badly dumbfounded. His hazel eyes went blank, and he shoved his hat back and scratched his tow head. "Well, hell, Bill! Don't I been treating you right! You ain't mad at me about somedings, was you? You don't mean you was quitting for goot?"

"I'm afraid I do, Pete. But it isn't because of anything you've done. It's just that I'm through in this country, Pete. Something I've been watching for a long time is coming to a head, and when it's over I'll shift on to other ranges. Right now, I'm going up to work for Lispy Louie, for a while. But I won't be coming back to the Circle G."

Gulick shook his head in utter bewilderment. "You was go to work mit Lispy Louie! Well, I be damned! Was you going cuckoo, Bill?"

Stagg laughed harshly. "Not yet, Pete. That's the story, if anybody should get curious: I've gone to work for Lispy Louie. The Crazy L happens to be headquarters for some things I want to find out, that's all. I'll be seeing you again, some day—I hope. Take care of yourself, Pete."

"Yah. You do der same. You—ach! Good-bye, Bill!"

He sat motionless, watching till Stagg passed from sight on the horse the big man had gotten from Stokes.

Stagg himself was thinking grimly of what Gulick had told him. If Kurt and Louie had gone to the doc's house, Mordan would tell Louie, Stagg was bound for the Crazy L. Louie would probably beat him to it.

Louie did. Here something needs be said of the queer, twisted being that was Lispy Louie le Grande. Louie was crooked; he admitted it himself, to himself. But he didn't consider that his especial brand of crookedness was of a criminal complexion. He thought it was smart; he couldn't help feeling that he was being slick if he got out of life and men a little more than he paid for, whatever the coin of purchase.

If he went to the store to buy beans and bacon, he always managed to walk away with a handful of dried prunes or nails or something of the sort in the pocket of his baggy coat.

If he went to a man's barn to borrow a rope or a shovel, he always managed to walk off with an old horseshoe, or a harness strap that wasn't quite worn out, or anything that looked usable or interesting, and he never failed to return the rope or shovel. Any bright or mysterious object was especially likely to fall prey to Louie's hungry fingers. Louie had never heard the word "kleptomaniac"; had he ever heard it he would have known what he was.

He had to steal. That was Louie's percentage from life, and everybody knew it, and the men of the Seco range were vastly irritated by it. Every one of them deep down inside had a sneaking resentment toward Lispy Louie. The man was a weird combination of virtues and faults, in which he wasn't too much different from all his fellows. He was different in the kind of faults and virtues he displayed, not in their possession.

Louie would steal anything easily portable that he could get his fingers on, yet Louie would give you the shirt off his back if you didn't mind its being patched and faded, which all of his shirts were, because he used strong soap and too much of it, and he always patched torn places, but he was no expert at the job.

He bathed in his creek twice a week the year round. His cabin was rough, but it was clean. He was clean. You might feel like kicking Louie's baggy pants because he stole anything he could filch the minute your back was turned, but you couldn't hate him. Nobody had ever hated him. Nobody had ever had much use for him either. And he wasn't to be blamed that he took Bill

Stagg's tolerance and compassion for friendliness and liking. He was shrewd in many ways, but his brain was slow. And nobody could read easily Bill Stagg's still black eyes.

So, thinking that Bill felt an emotion that had never touched Bill, or Louie either for that matter, he nearly rode the legs off the flea-bitten grey after he changed the saddle and bridle from the Arabian, and put the Arabian up carefully in the doctor's little barn back of the house, and left Arroyo behind.

He was so eager to reach the ranch ahead of Bill that the grey horse was worn to a whisper by the time he was allowed to rest in the home barn. But Louie didn't waste much sympathy on the animal. He had got there ahead of Bill. And he was so delighted about that that he gave the horse an extra good rubbing down, and fed him and watered him.

Then Louie went into the house to wait for Bill. He waited for over an hour, and the sun had set, before Bill finally came. The last light of the sun had gone, stars and moon were claiming the sky, and Louie had lighted a lamp, before he heard Bill ride up to the rough, clean little cabin and come up on the narrow little porch. Louie swung wide the door with open eagerness on his greasy dark face.

Now, it is practically an inviolable law of life that if some one or some thing, like a horse or a child, or a woman or a dog, bestows on you a free and unstinted worship, you cannot escape some faint feeling of responding warmth. Lispy Louie wasn't too much above the intelligence of a smart horse, the shrewdness of a cur that has been kicked from "here to Jericho" and learned thereby how to fend for itself—or the complete trust and gullibility of a little child who hasn't yet learned what it's all about. And Bill Stagg was a product of frustrated hopes and broken dreams and lost years, and he had a soft spot that could be touched.

And little greasy Louie swung open the door to Bill's knock, and looked up into Bill's face, far up, to Bill's astounding height, and touched that vulnerable spot with four words.

"Welcome home, old-timer!"

Bill stood still and thought of Micky. "Welcome home." And "old-timer" has the grace of affection and indulgence. But he thought more of the ring in Lispy Louie's voice, the excited light in Louie's one good eye. He stepped slowly inside the cabin.

"Doc told you I was coming, Louie?"

"The girl told me. How'd you know I wath in Arroyo?"

Bill told him about seeing Pete Gulick. "And Kurt, Louie?"

"Ain't hurt bad at all, Bill. Jutht got to retht for a few dayth. You thit down. I got thome thwell

126

grub I been keepin' hot for you. I'll get it right on the table. You hungry?"

Stagg wasn't. He was too weary to be hungry. But Lispy Louie had struck that vulnerable spot, and a slow smile lighted the huge man's face as he answered. "Hungry as the devil, Louie. You're sure a swell scout to take all this trouble for me."

"That ain't nothin'! Thit down, right here at the table. Gi' me your hat. You like coffee, Bill? Or will you take whithky?"

Stagg eased his great frame to a seat by Louie's small table. He thought the whisky was safer. "I guess I'll take whisky, Louie. If it won't rob you."

"Thay—what you talkin' about! You can have anything I got. Thith ith fine whithky, too. You take a good drink of it while I get your grub on the table, Bill."

He scurried about like a squirrel, bringing the bottle and a small thick glass. He planked them down in front of Stagg, and the big man helped himself to a long deep draught—from the bottle. In almost no time Louie had heaped before him a surprising repast of dandelion greens with bacon, beefsteak an inch thick and tender, and corn bread rich with pork fat and nut meats from the walnut tree in Louie's back yard. The steak was stripped with ham made from the same pig that had supplied the bacon for the greens and the fat for the corn bread.

Louie always had pigs around somewhere. And he sat and watched Stagg devour the food, and glowed till his greasy face gleamed.

"I thure hope it didn't get thpoiled from waitin', Bill."

"Spoiled? I haven't eaten such grub in a long time. You're a grand cook, Louie." Louie was. "And you certainly know how to cure pork. Say, Louie. I'd like to work here for you for a while. What do you say?"

"You, work for me? That'th cock-eyed. Nobody ever worked for me. Nobody ever wanted to. You got a good job on the Thircle G. But I—" He caught himself hastily. "I thure would be glad to have you around. You mean it?"

"Yes. I mean it, Louie. I'd like to stay here for a while. I don't know—maybe only a few days, Louie. Maybe much longer. Louie, do you know anything about where that Cottrelle fellow went?"

Louie shook his head. "Nope. I don't. That'th damn funny, too. I never thaw him. Lon never thaw him. He never come around here at all. Why?"

Stagg told him about Barnes. "And he got pretty damned close to the L I, Louie. I know, because I deliberately followed him all the way from Seco Springs. I saw him pass that stone marker Lon has built for the western edge there by the road. Up to there, it's anybody's road,

Louie. Beyond there it's Lon's road, and it doesn't lead anywhere else. I'm going to be damned curious to know whether Barnes gets to the L I. But there's no use speculating any more about that to-night. It will take a few days to tell the tale. I'm so damned glad Kurt wasn't badly hurt that I can't think of anything else much."

"Tho am I! Bill, I got thomethin' to tell you about Kurt." And rapidly, eagerly, he repeated what he had said to Kurt Quillan, and he saw Stagg's face turn from an expressionless paled mask to a ruddy, excited human face alive with interest. "You and me, Bill. We can get that jathper in a corner; we've got to. Do we work together, Bill?"

"We do," answered Stagg. He remembered telling Mordan that he didn't like Louie either, and he thought that perhaps he had spoken a bit hastily; Louie wasn't a bad little duck, when you got under his hide.

Only, the shoe was on the other foot; it was Louie who had got under Stagg's hide, and once you strike the vulnerable spot you can go deep, if you follow your lead. Queer little Louie was following his lead without any designing intent of doing so. Stagg's black eyes were almost indulgent as they rested on Louie's greasy face. "But you are keeping the key pieces hidden, Louie; and we won't get very far that way. What ranch is it that will come to Kurt when he is of age?"

If Louie's greasy face could have gone any whiter, it would have been startling; it bleached so suddenly. His voice lowered, and shook. "Bill, you got to promith me that—"

"Louie, I never double-crossed any man yet," Stagg interrupted, and his black eyes held steadily on the little man's frightened face. "If I tell you what Bess Quillan was to me, maybe you'll understand why I couldn't play you false, if you were minded to work with me as you offered to do." And when he had finished telling Louie the story of the frustrated love that had led him to the Seco range, little Louie blinked, and cleared his throat, and his one good eye looked away.

"I gueth I'd be pretty low if I didn't come clean with you, Bill. I never thought you liked me that much. The ranch ith the L-Over-Eth, Bill. Funny Lem never told Kurt that it wath hith by righth, ain't it?"

"How do you know this, Louie?"

"Well—I—oh, hell. I ain't goin' to keep nothin' from you. Wait a minute." Louie was pretty white again, but there was spirit in the little warped man, and determination. "I'll get it for you, Bill. I got to thee that it'th kept hid all the time."

He rose from the table, and went to the rude stone fireplace, across the room from the old iron stove. He climbed up the wall ladder beside the fireplace, till he had reached the few boards laid loosely across the bare poles which were his ceiling joists. He stood upon the nearest joist, reached up and pulled one of the stones out of the flue. From the hole behind the place where the loose stone had been, he took a small iron box. From the face of the box depended a broken hasp. Louie returned the stone to its place and came back down the ladder with the little iron box in his hand.

He set the box on the table in front of Stagg. "Jutht look in there." His voice was hoarse, but he was not wavering in his determination, though fear patently gripped him. He flipped back the lid of the iron box.

In it reposed two old papers, thumbed and soiled. Stagg picked them up together, and found them still very legible. The first was a deed, rude, made after the fashion of deeds in those wild and open countries in that day, but perfectly legal; showing that Bess Quillan had purchased, paying the entire purchase price in cash, the ranch here designated by certain markers and boundaries. The final sentence designating the name of the ranch had been printed by hand in capitals, that the established name of the purchased property might stand clear.

The second document was a wedding certificate; Bess Quillan had married Lon Ivey. There could be no possible doubt of the validity or legality of either document. Stagg raised his eyes to the flue of the fireplace, close to the low roof beyond the bared joists, where the small iron box with its broken hasp had reposed in secret.

"What are these two documents doing together, Louie? The certificate which proves Bess was Lon's wife, and the deed that proves Bess had bought the L-Over-S! And the L-Over-S lying all the way across the open range to the south-east, and Lem and his wife living there as if it were their own all these years! And the deed states plainly that Bess had bought the ranch in trust for Kurt, to become his property when he became of age, if he still lived, and to revert to her in case of his death. Could Kurt know this? Can that be why he shot Lem?"

"No thir!" objected Louie violently. "Becauthe I told Kurt motht of thith mythelf, and he didn't know a thing about it. Lem never did tell him! And thee here, Ivey didn't want him to know either. If Kurt died before he wath of age, and Lon had proof that he wath Beth Quillan'th huthband, who'd own the L-Over-Eth?"

Stagg's breath sucked in, in a hard, startled gasp. "Why, Lon would, of course; the property would revert to Bess, Bess is dead, and Lon would be her only heir. By gad, Louie; this is bad! Lon and Lem have been holding something over each other's heads all these years, each of them determined to have that ranch and cheat Kurt out of his just dues. If we can find out what

132

they were holding over each other, we can clean this mess out to the last dirty corner."

"Yeah," agreed Louie dryly, "but it'th goin' to be thome job! Lem'th dead, and Ivey won't talk. Mutht have been thomethin' pretty rotten between them two all thith time, any way you take it. What wath Lon doin' with the deed to the L-Over-Eth? That'th what I want to know. How did he ever get it away from Lem?"

"Louie!" Stagg returned the two documents to the box and closed down the box lid. "How do you come to have this box? Where did you get it? How long have you had it?"

Louie's cocked eye rolled again, and the good eye veered away, and his dark greasy face looked a little sheepish. "Well, you—you know how I kind of jutht take thingth thometimeth."

A fleeting sardonic smile crossed Stagg's black eyes. "Yes, I'm afraid everybody on the range knows how you just kind of take things sometimes. You mean to tell me that's the way you got this box?"

Louie nodded. "After that Cottrelle fella come up thith way, and nobody heard anything more about him, I thort of got curiouth to know if he really did come to the L I. Tho I thneaked over there a couple of dayth later when Lon and hith boyth wathn't around, and took a look to thee if there wath any thign that he'd been around there. I took a good look, too, all through the houthe

133

and through the barn. I didn't find no trathe of Cottrelle anywhere, but I did find that old iron box thtuck away back in a corner on a thelf, covered with thome old clothing. And I thought it looked kind of queer—tho I—I jutht took it. And I brought it home, and pried it open, and that'th what wath in it.

"After I looked at the paperth, I dug that rock looth and hid 'em up there, tho Lon couldn't pothibly come rootin' around here and find 'em. I better put 'em away now. You've theen 'em, and that'th enough."

He picked up the box, and Stagg watched in silence while the little man returned box and papers to the hole behind the rock, and as Louie came back from the ladder to his seat beside the table, Stagg's eyes were burning with excitement.

"Louie, there is more back of this than you've thought of yet! It has something to do with Bess's death. It has something to do with both Cottrelle and Barnes. Doc's wrong. They were both looking for Lon Ivey and there was no bluff about it! Why Cottrelle never showed himself to Lon is something that may be no mystery at all; maybe he didn't want Lon to see him. Maybe he was simply looking for something he didn't find. Doc said he'd bet me Barnes never would show up at the L I either. I'm ready to bet now that doc's right. Barnes doesn't want Lon to get sight of him, either. Listen, Louie; did you ever take a good slant at your branding iron? Do you remember just how it looks?"

Stagg could see the iron in his mind's eye, as he had seen it hanging on Louie's barn wall, two L's boxed together, so:

⌐⌐

Louie stared at him. "Well, I ought to remember how it lookth! I made it mythelf!"

"I know you did." Stagg's gaze held his steadily. "And it's no more a crazy L than I am. It's an L down and an L up, but you've got a right to call it a Crazy L if you want to. Nobody needs to remind you what Lon's L I brand looks like, either. Doesn't take much of a stroke with a running iron to make that L I into your Crazy L, Louie—just one little left-hand swipe at the top of the I."

Louie shrank as if Stagg had struck him, and the cocked eye rolled wildly, like a signal of dire distress. "I never done nothin' like that in my life, Bill! I know Lon thayth I did, but it'th a lie!"

"I'd really like to believe that, Louie." Something like an answering distress showed on Stagg's smooth dark face, rumbled in his deep resonant voice. "But when Lon said that in Seco Springs, several weeks ago, the word was repeated to me. It didn't sound like you. I never figured that you'd swipe anything bigger than what you could pack home in one hand, but I didn't consider it was much of my business, and I had no intention of sticking my face into it. A few days after that, I was looking up some of Pete's strays, you know they're always coming over your way.

"I went across the upper corner of your ranch, and so help me Heaven, Louie, I passed a couple of Lon's whitefaces herding along with your handful of Durhams, and the L I brand on them had been changed to your Crazy L with a running iron. I could tell it a mile off. And when I came back with the strays, I saw some single-handed branding going on, right there on your land. But I kept my mouth shut and rode on. I didn't like it; I didn't like to see you get started on anything like that. But don't tell me you didn't do it, Louie; because I saw you at it with my own eyes."

Louie was pasty white, and his mouth was quivering, but the look on his face was not that of a man caught in a lie or a criminal act; it was the look of a rather simple-minded small boy unjustly denounced and disgraced in the eyes of his hero. His voice was so hoarsened that it was harsh, but it remained steady.

"How you know it wath me?"

Stagg's slow smile was pitying, mildly mocking. "I'd know that old tan hat of yours anywhere, Louie; and your faded-blue shirts, and those ragged old red chaps you're wearing right

136

now. It was pretty dumb of you to think you could conceal your identity by wearing a red bandanna over your face, and not having sense enough to ditch those chaps and that old hat that's like a signboard."

Louie straightened, and his mouth quivered again. His one good eye flamed with eagerness and protest. "I tell you it wathn't me! What'd happen to me if thith got out, and you or thomebody elthe would thwear you theen me runnin' my brand on Lon'th cattle, and the whole range took it theriouth and believed it? What'd happen to me, huh?"

Stagg's smile died, and his dark features turned a little hard. "No two ways about that, Louie. We don't want rustling to start on this range. The boys would just get together and take one look at those reworked whitefaces and string you up to the nearest tree as an example to the next fellow not to try it. That's why I kept my mouth shut. I'm awfully slow about saying things I can't take back, especially when somebody else's life's in the question. I knew if you kept it up long enough, somebody else would see you and tell on you, and it would be stopped without my meddling in it. And I was hoping you'd get wise to yourself and quit it in time."

"I—never—done—it!" said Lispy Louie. "And I never thtarted no fight with Kurt the mornin' he killed Lem Thtrickland, either. I wath helpin'

Jerry Hulan round up thome more of Pete'th thtrayth. Jerry wath thtill here with me when you found Lem and took him home; he'd already been here a couple of hourth."

"Oh, yes. I know that. Jerry told me, because I asked him if he'd seen anything of Kurt, and he said he'd been over here with you. Nobody's accusing you of starting a fight with Kurt. That'd be silly."

"Oh, would it!" Poor little Louie shivered in a blend of fear and triumph. "Then you jutht athk Kurt! It wath a man drethed like me, and Kurt thought it wath me till I proved to him it wathn't! You go right down to Arroyo and athk him! Bill, anybody could get hold of an old hat and red chapth like mine."

Stagg's deep black eyes dilated in unmistakable astonishment. The entire expression of his face changed. For the first time, he considered the idea that the figure he had seen was not Lispy Louie. And his relief at the proof Louie offered warmed his dark face from mere pity to swiftly rising championing defence. That thing in him which couldn't bear to see an under dog kicked flowered almost hotly.

"Why, that's a damned dirty piece of business, Louie! Somebody's trying to frame you! It doesn't take much brain to see through that, old-timer. Somebody's trying to make the rest of the range believe you've gone clean bad. Trying to get you strung up for rustling. Trying to get you shot by Kurt Quillan.

"Whoever he was, he had no intention of killing Kurt. He took a shot or two at Kurt from ambush, so Kurt wouldn't get a chance to shoot him down, letting Kurt get just a flash of those clothes, so Kurt would think it was you and go gunning for you."

Louie shivered again, this time wholly sick from fear. "Yeah, and it come near workin', too! That'th why Kurt wath hangin' around up here when I thaw him and come and told you. I'll never know why he didn't lay me cold when I come up to him with your methage."

"He can probably answer that. It doesn't matter much right now, Louie. What does matter is that somebody's got it in for you, and we've got to find out who it is, and why he wants to get rid of you. It could be Lon, Louie. He probably suspects that you took that box, and he's about your size, and he has black hair like you."

"Yeah, I thought of that," admitted Louie honestly, "but it won't work. Lon thought that I took the box, all right, and he come over here and looked all around. I thaw him, only he didn't know I wath watchin' him. I gueth maybe he thtill thinkth it, but the reathon he thinkth I thwiped hith cattle ith becauthe he thaw thomebody drethed like me doin' it. He thaid that, but I never believed he thaw no thuch

139

perthon before. I do now, though. I got to believe it. Lon thaw the thame fella you and Kurt both thaw. But who ith he, and what'th he got it in for me for?"

"Keep your head, Louie." In that moment Bill Stagg came as near to feeling real liking for Louie le Grande as any man had ever done; the poor little devil, being preyed upon by some slick crook, because he was an outcast of the range, disliked for his small thieveries, ripe suspect for anybody's trap.

Stagg reached out and laid a steadying hand on Louie's thin shoulder. "I'm with you, old-timer. We'll get to the bottom of this. We've got to plan ahead, and know just where we're stepping, too. And we have to work fast, because whoever is behind all this mix-up isn't going to let any grass grow under his feet. You keep out of sight. You stick close at home, and you leave off those damned old chaps of yours when you're out riding around your range. No—I guess you'd better not. You keep right on in your regular way of things, only you stay close. There are three people I'm going to see right away: Kurt Quillan, Lon Ivey, and Pete Gulick."

"What for, Bill?"

"Now, don't go letting your imagination run away with you, Louie. I want to learn anything I can find out from Lon, but I'm not going to give you away. I want to make Kurt do a little talking, but I'm not going to tell him all this dirt we've raked up yet. And Pete Gulick knows a man in Chicago, a lawyer, John McNary. I know Chicago's a whaling big town, but McNary's a lawyer; and lawyers get to know a lot of people. I'm going to get Pete to write to McNary and see if McNary ever heard of Cottrelle or Barnes. I'm going to start out before daylight. I'll see Pete and Kurt first, and leave Lon till I come back. I want to know everything I can learn before I tackle Lon.

"And see here, Louie: have you got nerve enough to do a little snooping around while I'm gone, to see if you can get any line on Barnes and what he's up to?"

Louie's dark face had gained back a little of its colour. He was limp with relief at having won Stagg's trust, but he sat up and squared his shoulders. "I ain't got much nerve, but I'll do it. I been hatin' Lon becauthe I thought he wath tryin' to do me dirt and cheat Kurt out of gettin' the L-Over-Eth. But thinthe you and I've been talkin', I'm beginnin' to believe I wath wrong. Lon ain't to blame for thayin' I wath brandin' hith cattle when he really thought he thaw me doin' it. And maybe he wath thavin' that deed to try to protect Kurt from thomethin' Lem wath tryin' to pull on Kurt. I gueth I done Lon wrong, Bill."

"Yes, it looks like it, Louie. But you keep those papers hidden and you keep your mouth shut till

141

I come back. We'll know more then, and Kurt's safe at Mordan's. I expect we'd better get to bed, Louie. I've thought so hard my head's tired. I'd give a good deal to know how Kurt's feeling."

CHAPTER IX

KURT RIDES AGAIN

KURT was feeling infinitely better. He was warmed and strengthened by the various foods Micky had made possible for him to get down in liquid form, and he was sound asleep. Micky was sitting by his bed, the lamp turned low, thinking, and dreaming, and wishing. Mordan stepped to the door and glanced in.

"Don't you think you'd better go to bed, Micky? You needn't have any fear of your patient trying to run away this time. He's going to remain right here where he's safe till we tell him he can go."

Micky raised her brooding amber eyes, and turned her head so quickly that even the dim lamplight made silver glints on her pale blonde hair. "No, I don't want to go to bed yet, Uncle Dan. I want him to have another meal before I leave him for the night. You've changed your mind about Kurt, haven't you, Uncle Dan?"

Mordan advanced slowly into the room, a troubled frown on his thin face. "Well, yes. I have.

142

Couldn't help it, the way he's been acting. I'd be inclined to think if a man wants to be redeemed, there has to be a way open. Though it might have a coffin at the end of it. Never forget that."

"I can't forget it." Pain and fear blended on her pale face. "I'm bitterly afraid of it. But if that must be the way, I'd rather see him die to clear the record, than to live to make a blacker one."

"I've got at least one thing to be proud of," said Mordan, "that you're of my blood. His is a pretty dark record already; it would take a lot of atoning or justification to set him right in the eyes of men, but he might have the sand to live through it. If he does, I could even get used to the idea of you loving him. And I couldn't say anything bigger than that."

"Nobody could say anything bigger than that, doctor." The voice came from the bed; the tight, strained voice of the outlaw, and both Micky and Mordan started and turned their heads, to see his eyes, still and clear, that clean cold blue, looking straight at them. "A man couldn't play for a bigger stake. But I haven't much hope of being able to win through. As you said, the record's pretty dark. I've killed, and I'm not going to try to deny it."

"See here, Kurt." Mordan approached the bed and stood looking down into Quillan's tense, drained face. "You told my niece that you killed Lem Strickland because he damned well deserved it. What had Lem Strickland done that he deserved death at your hands, after he'd brought you up, and been like a father to you?"

Quillan's blue eyes veiled, closed for an instant, then went from the doctor to Micky. When they again raised to the doctor's gaze, Kurt's face had been wiped of all expression, his voice was hard and level.

"I'll tell you the truth, all I know of it, and you can take it or leave it, or make what you like of it. First, I'm telling you what I learned from Lispy Louie." By this he meant Louie's astounding assertion that he was rightful heir to one of the best ranches on the Seco. He repeated what Louie had said, and went on evenly: "Now you can add this to it. The night before I got into that shooting affair with Lem, I sneaked into the ranch after dark. I'd about made up my mind to leave the country. I'd never had any quarrel with Lem; Mrs. Strickland had always acted as if she was half afraid of him, but he'd always been good to me.

"I just wanted to see him again, before I went away. I was going to tell him that this country was no place for me. I was going looking for a better one. I heard the sound of his voice, out beyond the barn, talking to somebody. I didn't want to run into anything there on Lem's ranch, so I slipped up a little closer to see who was there, and to see if I could find out how long he was

144

going to stick around. And I discovered that the two of them were having some pretty hot words.

"The other man was Lon Ivey, and he was trying to get Lem to do something. Lem was fighting mad. I heard him say, 'No, I won't do it! And if you don't realize it by this time, you're a bigger fool than I thought you were! I'm telling you for the last time, you hand it over or I'll have your hide!'

"And Ivey laughed, as ugly a sound as I ever heard from any man. And this is what he said: 'You make a move to pull anything, Lem Strickland, and I'll spread it all over this range that you killed Bess Quillan!'"

The doctor's thin face went blank, and Micky gasped and bent toward the bed, one hand flung out to grip Kurt's arm. "Kurt!"

Quillan's eyes swerved to meet her gaze, and the fire of rage began to cloud the clean blue. "That's what he said, Micky. And Lem didn't even deny it. He merely sneered, and dared Lon to go ahead and tell it. He said: 'You'd never make anybody believe it. Nobody knows it but you and me, and nobody ever will know it. I've guarded that secret too long, Lon. You'll meet me halfway and get this thing settled, if you know what's good for you. I'll kill you if I have to, but I'm giving you one last chance.'

"Lon flared back at him, but I'd heard enough. I got out of there. And the next day that fellow dressed like Lispy Louie opened fire on me, and Lem came barging in. And I remembered that night in the pass, all I do remember of it, my mother fighting with some man, screaming, and then the awful crash of a gun that I thought would split my head open.

"And then she was lying on the ground, and I was crouched by her, and I'll keep living over till I die that awful feeling when I saw her head all blood, and I screamed at her, and she wouldn't answer. I saw it again when Lem came riding up. I shot at the stranger and hit Lem, who came between us. In that minute I hated Lem as I never hated anything, and I wasn't sorry I shot him down by mistake. He had it coming. He killed her, and she'd never done anything to anybody. I don't know why Lem would take me and let me go on living after he'd killed her. I think it had something to do with the ranch. The ranch Louie means must be the L-Over-S. But the whole thing's too badly tangled up to be straightened out now."

"Maybe not," said the doctor quietly. "If we can get hold of this man who's dressing like Lispy Louie, running brands on Lon's cattle and firing on you, I've an idea we can find our answer, if we can make him talk, and there are usually ways to loosen even very reluctant tongues."

"Think of every man on this range that it could

be, Kurt." Micky's amber eyes burned with her intensity of thought as she reached over and turned up the lamp. "That ought to narrow it down. Lispy is small and thin, his hair is black, and there's that cocked eye when you get close to him. How many men do you know who could impersonate Louie at a little distance?"

"Not many," answered Kurt, thinking intently. "Small men are, after all, more common than really big men. There must be a half dozen around here that could pass for Louie in those clothes. Lon Ivey himself is one. And so is Frank Cross, who owns the Cross-Bar, right above the L-Over-S. Living next to Lem, I suppose he could be mixed up in it some way. But there's another one—and even to suggest him, and to suggest what might be behind him being the one, is going so far that I hate to put it into words. But he's Coke Laughlin, the foreman of the L-Over-S."

The doctor's lean face furrowed in a frown, and he pushed his grey hair back from his forehead, and sat down on the edge of the bed. "I'm afraid I don't get that, quite, Kurt."

Quillan's voice again sank to that level tonelessness. "Coke Laughlin could pass for Lispy Louie twenty feet away if he were dressed like Louie and his face was covered. Coke's face is handsome, and his black eyes are straight. There are just five men in this country who were here when Lem brought me to the L-Over-S.

They are Lon Ivey, Pete Gulick, Frank Cross, you yourself, doc, and from what he himself says, Bill Stagg. Coke came to the L-Over-S just a little while after Mrs. Strickland married Lem. And anybody could see that she'd known Coke before. Even I, little kid as I was, could tell it.

"And you could see that Coke thought she was about all there was. He never stopped thinking about it, and as I grew older I could see that she kind of shrank from Lem, and thought just about as much of Coke as he did of her. If she and Coke got their heads together, and got rid of both Lem and me, all she'd have to do would be to marry him, and he'd be owner of as good an outfit as a fellow could want. There it is in plain words. I warned you that it wasn't pretty."

"It's damned nasty," said Mordan tersely. "But if the L-Over-S is the ranch, it's a very likely solution. But if Coke is the man, what's his idea in trying to frame Lispy Louie?"

"That's too easy to need a second thought." A thin smile drove faint dimples into Quillan's cheeks. "Louie's the most logical goat on the whole range. If Coke gets people down on Louie, and Lon Ivey is found shot, who's going to be blamed for it? Lispy Louie, getting even with Lon for accusing him of cattle stealing; and if Coke is the man back of this business, he knows what kind of quarrel was between Lon and Lem, and he knows he has to get rid of Lon. It fits all the way around. If we could only be sure that the L-Over-S was the ranch."

The doctor's thin long body humped there on the edge of the bed, and his long, nervous hands gripped themselves between his knees. "I've an idea Louie will tell Bill Stagg all he knows, and I think Bill will be coming in pretty soon to check up on you. Suppose he corroborates your suspicion that it's the L-Over-S, Kurt?"

The outlaw's gaze turned to Micky's pale, delicate face, and one would have gotten the impression that he was straining his sight to peer far into the distance, toward something bright and fair, to reach which a man would risk and dare more than the mere essence of life.

"Then I'm going over there and get Coke Laughlin out in the blacksmith shop, and stay with him till I get it out of him," he replied.

"No, Kurt!" Micky's hand tightened on his arm. "That's the most dangerous place on the range for you, Lem's own ranch—"

"Maybe it's really my own ranch," Kurt cut in, his voice still level and toneless. "If it is, and they're trying to pull anything like that, they have to know just what they're doing, and they don't get away with it. The thing has to be cleaned up; maybe that's my path to the washed slate, and we'll never know if I don't find out. Bill Stagg is up there at the Crazy L trying to see what he can find out. I'm not low enough to be ungrateful, whatever his interest in me may be."

"I'm going to tell you what his interest in you is," Micky said steadily. "I don't believe he'd care. He told Uncle Dan and me. I don't believe he'd object to your knowing now. I'm willing to assume the full responsibility. It was your mother, Kurt."

The outlaw lay with his still clear eyes fixed steadily on her face, as she told him of Bill Stagg's lost love. Then a faint smile barely disturbed the dimples at the corners of his mouth.

"That makes all the more important what I was going to say. I can't lie here and let Bill Stagg or any other man settle my affairs and fight my battles. I'll wait just one more day, and get a little more strength, then I'm on my way. If Bill doesn't come by then, I'll hit for the Crazy L, and see Lispy Louie first. I have to know whether that ranch is the L-Over-S."

Micky rose and went out of the room, too shaken to speak, to prepare his food, and her mind was wholly occupied with one wild prayer—that Bill Stagg would come before it was too late.

Bill Stagg himself had gone to bed and to sleep. He kept his word to Louie, was up before daylight, ate a breakfast Louie eagerly prepared for him, and set off for the Circle G, straight across country to the east, on the horse he had got from Jay Stokes. He reached the Circle G shortly after nine o'clock that morning, to find Gulick out in the barn saddling a mount. The little

Dutchman's fat face was pale and tense with excitement. He greeted Stagg with explosive delight.

"By golly, Bill! Just de man I was wishing I couldt see. I got something to show you, yet. I was going in right away to see doc, and to send de answer from Arroyo. Look, Bill! Vot you t'ink of dot? Jerry Hulan brought it mit de mail last night."

He dragged from his pocket a thin business-looking envelope, extending it toward Stagg, and the first thing Stagg noted was the Chicago return address in the upper left-hand corner, and the name of John McNary. He removed the single typewritten sheet from the envelope, and ran his eyes down over the message.

"DEAR PETE GULICK:

"It has been some time since I have heard from you. I hope you are all well out there. I am writing you just now on important business, Pete.

"About two months ago we were commissioned by a Mr. Owen Barnes to secure information concerning his sister, Mrs. Bess Quillan, who came to the Seco range some years ago and disappeared. She had with her several thousand dollars insurance money which she had received on the death of her husband.

"Mr. Barnes had already unearthed this much when he came to us for help; he had been trying for years to find some trace of his sister, and of the small son who was with her at the time of her disappearance. He requested us to send a man out there to investigate. He could give us no clue, save that in the last letter his sister ever wrote him she mentioned a man named Alonzo Ivey; the letter was postmarked Madder Junction. Barnes wrote to Ivey at Madder Junction and the letter came back uncalled for. But Barnes thought the man might live in that territory somewhere. So we sent our man, Warren G. Cottrelle, out there.

"We have heard nothing from him since. Barnes grew uneasy at Cottrelle's long silence and decided to come there himself. He left with me instructions to make immediate efforts to get into communication with some one in your territory if I did not hear from him within two weeks. I told him I knew you, and would write you.

"But I decided against waiting any two weeks. If there is something wrong there, which I very much suspect, the time to be warned is right now. So I am writing to ask whether you can give me any light on the subject.

"Does this man Ivey live around there? Did Cottrelle ever arrive there? Is Barnes there now? If you can tell me nothing, I shall not risk sending another man out there to disappear. I'll come myself and see what's going on. I'll be obliged if you'll give me a quick answer.

"Yours, as ever,
"JOHN McNARY."

"So!" ejaculated Gulick, as Stagg folded and returned the letter. "Gifs it shenanigans, eh? I got de answer already written, yah. I go to mail it right now and tell doc."

Stagg was frowning blackly. "I guess it all clicks, Pete. Madder Junction was the closest railroad stop then, wasn't it?"

"Yah. De railroad don't come to Arroyo yet, it don't come to Arroyo for nearly two years after dot. Coming dis way by de railroad, you had to get off at Madder Junction, und come mit a horse by Lobo Pass. Und you had to go out der same way, if you was going by der railroad."

"But didn't people around here get mail at Seco Springs, then?" said Stagg. "It came in by stage from the south, didn't it? Why would Bess go all the way to Madder Junction to mail a letter to her brother, when she could have as well taken it to Seco Springs? She must have sent it there by some one else, so Lon wouldn't know about it."

"Hey, vait a minute!" Gulick's hazel eyes bored into Stagg's face. "You was holding out on me, yet! What's Lon got to do mit it?"

"She was Lon's wife, Pete. Come on, let's get going. I'll take Skater, as long as I'm here, and turn this nag back to Stokes. I've learned several things, Pete. We'll talk as we go. But I want to reach doc's place as quickly as possible. Kurt's there, and I have to talk to him. I left Louie keeping an eye open to see whether or not he could get track of Barnes. Louie's not as big a fool as some people think he is. Going back to that letter, Pete, I suppose the reason that Barnes's letter to Ivey was returned uncalled for was that Ivey got his mail at Seco Springs then, and very probably wasn't known in Madder Junction at all."

"Yah, dot would be it. Himmel, what a mess! He wasn't known very vell anywhere around here at dot time. I think he don't been here more as a couple of years or so, and he was away across de range dere. But he vas a nice fella. I don't like seeing him get mixed up in such a bizness. Und Bess was his vife! I bet you I wouldn't want to be de skunk what killed Bess, if Lon ever finds it out!" The fat little Dutchman was forced to break into a trot, to keep up with Stagg, who turned abruptly and started out of the barn dragging his saddled horse behind him.

Stagg brought Skater out of the corral, and Gulick stood waiting while Stagg shifted the riding gear from Stokes's horse to his own. As Stagg tightened the cinch around Skater's white belly, he glanced across the horse's back at Gulick.

"What did you tell McNary in your answer, Pete?"

"Oh, I just told him what we know about Bess, und how Cottrelle vas come, und send de pinto back, und how Barnes just got here. Himmel! I wonder if I better open de letter und tell him dot she vas married mit Lon? What you think?"

"I think you'd better hold the letter up till we talk to doc and Kurt, Pete. There are several things you'll want to add. Well, we might as well get going. We can reach Arroyo pretty close to noon, if we fan the nags on the tail."

They reached Arroyo shortly after twelve-thirty, put up the horses in Stokes's barn, and went across the street to find Micky and the doctor sitting at lunch at a table in Kurt's room. Kurt, Mordan explained, had insisted on dressing and getting up to eat. The doctor had removed the wires from Kurt's jaws that morning, and Quillan insisted that he must celebrate, but Mordan wanted him to be out of sight of casual callers, so he had brought a larger table into the bedroom.

Kurt rose and stretched himself to his height, and gave Stagg a strange, quick smile, and said that though his side was sore and his jaw stiff, he could have soft foods and he was beginning to feel nearly human again.

Stagg looked at him, at the clean cold eyes, the finely chiselled face, and something hurt within, sharply, so that the huge man winced; Bess's boy. He said harshly:

"We've come to talk to you, Kurt. Something almighty important has happened. Show him that letter, Pete. And you pass it around to doc and Micky when you're through reading it, Kurt. Sit down, Pete. You look like you were ready to fly to pieces."

"Yah. Don't I? By Jiminy, I feel dot vay!" Pete dropped into a chair and mopped his round face. Micky insisted that Stagg and Gulick must eat, that there was plenty of food left, and rose to set places for them, while Stagg sat motionless, watching Kurt read the letter.

As Kurt came to the end of the missive, he raised his gaze to meet Stagg's intent stare, and there passed between them something of that first communion between men who have gone through deeps together. The outlaw's dark skin was as nearly pallid as it could grow, and the clear-blue of his eyes was like ice in the sunshine.

"What is it, son?" asked Stagg steadily.

"Micky says you saw Lem pick me up in his arms that night my mother was killed, Bill?" answered Quillan, as he passed the letter to Mordan without looking at him.

"Himmel, Bill! Was you dere?" Gulick cried sharply.

No one paid any attention to him. The doctor took the letter, and Micky came to stand by him and read it with him. Quillan's attention was centred on Stagg, oblivious of everything else for that tense moment.

"But he killed her, Bill; Lem did." And he told the huge man how he came to know that grim fact. "What was it Lon had that Lem wanted? We have to find out!"

"I can tell you right now, Kurt. It's the deed to the L-Over-S. Only Lon hasn't it any more. Louie's got it, and he's got it safe." He went on to reveal to Quillan all he had learned. "It looks pretty open and shut, Kurt. Lon knew that Lem was trying to cheat you out of the ranch. All these years he's been holding the deed, evidently intending to make Lem come through when you arrived at legal age, holding over Lem's head the threat of telling that Lem had killed Bess."

"Oh, it doesn't seem possible!" Micky cried sharply. "Be careful that you aren't jumping to some awful conclusion that will trap the wrong man. How could Lem have been as base as that? Remember how he walked all the way to the Seven Up that night, carrying Kurt, bringing Bess's body on his own horse. And Bill saw that! Bill knows that's true! A man who could show that much fineness of feeling couldn't be so bad as you're making him seem to be! I can't help it; I have a sure intuition that you're putting things together that don't fit."

"But Lem practically admitted that he killed her, Micky." Quillan's straight gaze sought her face, puzzled. He had too much respect for her judgment and penetration to view anything she said with the least casual attention; if Micky said it, it had weight and substance, it was to be taken seriously and given concentration and consideration. Yet this statement she had made seemed to be the essence of paradox. "A man with fineness of feeling couldn't shoot a woman twice, Micky, the way he shot her. Maybe he was sorry for it afterward, maybe that was why he picked me up and carried me. Maybe it wasn't the kind of remorse that lasts very long."

"I don't know what it may have been, Kurt." Micky stood straight before him, and he rose and poised towering lithely above her, looking down into her face. "But if we ever know the straight of it, you will find that I am right. Something here doesn't fit."

"No, I guess it doesn't," Kurt admitted, and although he was aware of every eye in the room watching him with an intent kind of curiosity, yet he was still in a way conscious of her gaze only. "So I'll have to dig up the pieces that will fit, from wherever they are."

"Kurt, you're not going over to the L-Over-S!" Micky's cry was almost angry, yet there was in it also a chord of fear nearly as high as the anger.

"I certainly am, Micky. I'm going to-night, as soon as I can get my horse saddled, and Coke Laughlin will tell me what I want to know before I'm through with him."

"Uncle Dan!" Micky whirled to her uncle, and Mordan uncoiled his long lean body to a standing posture. "Uncle Dan—don't let him go—"

"I'm afraid there's no stopping him, my dear." The doctor laid a steadying arm across her shoulders. "He's lost a little blood, and he'll have to take a little punishment in barging right out like this, but it won't kill him. Besides, he's quite right, and I wouldn't stop him if I could. If a man wants to be redeemed, nobody has a right to hinder his earning that right. Let him go, and give him your blessing, and pray for him. Where are his guns, Bill?"

"Over at Jay Stokes's barn," Stagg got to his huge height, with his arresting lightness of motion, and his black eyes burned. "And, by gad, if he has that brand of courage, I'm going over and get them for him. Go saddle your Arabian, Kurt; I'll bring the guns, and my belts. Your belts are still at the pass. I'll be back with them by the time you're ready to leave."

"Ride 'em, cowboy!" The little fat Dutchman leaped up, fairly quivering with excitement. "I bet you we do somethings now, by golly! Kurt, you sit down, yet. You take it easy till you got to take on der chin. I go saddle dot horse."

Without waiting for any answer, Gulick strode out of the room, Stagg only a few feet behind him, and Mordan glanced from Kurt to Micky —and followed Gulick toward the kitchen, and on out to the barn.

The two remaining in the room stood just as they had been standing, face to face, looking into

159

each other's eyes. Quillan's colour burned high in his cheeks, but his cold blue eyes were wiped clean of all expression, save for that faint impression of a man striving to peer through the distance to some fair bright thing infinitely far away. His voice was tight and hard, as though it hurt when it forced its way through his throat. He said steadily:

"You are the first girl I ever saw that I wanted. I'd do anything to make of myself what you'd like me to be. You've been kind. If you meant it only as kindness, I want to know now. If there isn't any chance you could care the way I've learned to care, I don't want to go on blundering along in the dark, hoping for something I can never have."

"It wasn't—" Micky's lips whitened at the edges, but she held her head high. "I wasn't just being kind. You're the only man I ever wanted, too. I know the odds you're facing, but I still say that it's worth any cost to have you come out of it with the score clean. And if that takes you out of this world, there's another world waiting. And I'll meet you there, some day."

She lifted her face, and raised her hands to his shoulders. "Kurt!" She was offering her lips, and his face quivered from cheek bone to chin as he drew back.

"No. Not yet! Not till I've won out. Maybe never—but not yet!"

He snatched up his blue beaver hat, hanging on the back of a chair, and went out of the room, weaving a little, as if he were drunk, or perhaps slightly blinded and unable to see his way.

Micky dropped into the chair whereon the hat had hung, and buried her face in her hands, and through her shaking sobs she heard the echo of her uncle's voice saying: "Nobody has a right to hinder his earning that right."

They had spent the entire afternoon talking, and she noted dully as she raised her head that the dusk was falling.

CHAPTER X

THE WEB TIGHTENS

KURT QUILLAN rode away from the doctor's house that night as he had never ridden on any mission before with those heavy guns hanging at his thighs, and in the doctor's back yard three men stood watching his figure disappear into the shadows of the falling dusk, while inside the house a girl rose and brushed the tears from her pale, tired face.

When Kurt and the brown Arabian had quite faded from sight, Stagg broke the silence that had held there in the back yard. "Well, Pete, you'd better come into doc's house and write a postscript to that letter you're sending McNary. Then we'll go on."

"Where was you go now, Bill?"

"Straight back to the Crazy L, to see what Louie's found out, and to talk to Lon Ivey," Stagg answered as he led the way up the steps. Inside the front room, he turned to speak to Mordan, who was laying out pen and ink on the table for little Pete Gulick. "Doc, if Kurt gets back here before I do, you tell him to wait for me. Seems like this business is taking a lot of riding and talking, but there's no help for it. We can't any of us afford to go off half-cocked and crack down on the wrong man. Somehow I kind of agree with Micky. It don't just seem that Coke Laughlin is the man, that that's the answer to it. There's a lot we have to find out yet, and we're going at it the best way we know."

Micky came quietly in from the bedroom, and Stagg turned with quick deference, and with a peculiar air of some kinship between them, as she walked up to him.

"Bill, will you do one thing for me?"

"Anything I can, Micky. You just name it."

"Will you ask Kurt when you see him again why he didn't make any attempt to shoot Lispy Louie when Louie came up to him with your message? I wanted to ask him—and I couldn't. And I have a feeling that it's important. Will you please be sure to ask him?"

"Why, of course, if you want me to." Stagg's gaze was puzzled. "That seems like a small thing to be very important, but I'll certainly ask him. And on the other hand, it mightn't be a bad thing to ask Lispy himself why he wasn't afraid of Kurt. He tried to make me think he was when he came over to the Circle G after me that day. But he wasn't. He wasn't afraid till afterward, when he learned from Kurt that Kurt was up there after him. I found that out from talking to Louie himself, but Louie didn't realize it."

"I don't believe that's so important," Micky replied, "but it may be. Anything we can find out may be the one thing we need to know."

"Well, I got him all done now." Pete Gulick corked the ink bottle and rose, folding his letter. "Much obliged for de new envelope, doc. I sure ripped dot von all to smiddereens. I told him everything what is. Und I told him we write him somethings more in a few days, yet, and tell him what happens, and if it don't happen, we write him anyways."

"Sounds as if you didn't leave anything out, Pete." Stagg gave his late boss a broad, humorous smile. "I guess we're ready to go, then. Thanks for everything, doc. And you, Micky. Maybe I can pay you back some day. You never can tell. Come on, Pete."

After they had left the doctor's house, the huge man with the frosted black hair, astride his white horse, and the little fat Dutchman, leading the Seven Up horse which he was going to return to Pat Ryan for Stagg, rode in silence till Arroyo was lost in the night behind them. The little Dutchman was hunting around in his disordered mind for words and he wasn't segregating them with any great facility. So that, after all, he said badly the thing which most distressed him, blurting it out in the first words that came handy to his tongue.

"Himmel, Bill! Dot's a fine kettle of fish, yah! Dot sweet Micky in luff mit a killer, und der killer mit der idea dot he's going to reform yet, when it's too late altogedder! He ain't got a chance! Der next rancher dot takes a crack at him won't be so easy on him like Ivey done. Gifs it a smack right between der eyes yet, and dot's der end of Mister Kurt Quillan!"

"Yes, it does look pretty hopeless," agreed Stagg, and even in the dark, perhaps because of the dark that magnified sound and inflection, the regret and pain in the deep bass voice was like a minor strain. "But if he tries hard enough, and proves clearly enough that he wants to live as a man should, and comes through it alive, maybe the men of the Seco can cross off what he's done and give him a new lease. I don't know, Pete. I know you could do it, and I know I could."

"Oh, sure, sure! We take him by der hand und say, 'We forgiff you, so long as you don't do it some more.' But I don't know about der other fellers. I told mine hands to lay off him until we see what it is, but I just got a sneakin' idea dot ven mine back is turned, if Kurt comes along, dey forgets vot I say, and remember dose fellers he was killed, und start shootin'. Und I couldn't blame dem. Dot was a purty terrible thing, when he shoots Lem Strickland."

"Yes. Damned bad. The more I think of what Micky said, the more I'm afraid she's right. Women feel things like that, I've noticed. Your wife does, Pete. You know Lena's always getting what she calls 'feelings,' and, by gad, they may not seem to have any basis, but nineteen times out of twenty, she's right. And Micky's seeing the holes in this solution we've all cooked up, she's seeing the fine edges that won't dovetail. I—I'm afraid it's a mistake about Lem Strickland shooting Bess, Pete. I can't quite make myself believe that he did it."

"*Nein.* Neither could I. If Kurt had waited just a liddle longer, he might haf heard more what was said mit Lon and Lem, und haf got der straight of it. Just hearing a schmidgin of a conversation ain't always what it sounds like, already. Well, I think I turn off here, Phil, und take a short cut by der hills. You was go straight by der Crazy L, *nein*?"

"Straight as Skater can travel. Do all you can to make those boys of yours keep their hands off their guns if they should happen to run across Kurt, Pete. If I turn up anything I'll let you know. If you run into anything of importance, send one of the boys after me; I'll be at the Crazy L for a day or two anyway."

"Yah, I do dot, sure, Bill! Keep der upper lip mit a stiffness, und don't stick der chin out. I see you in church."

Stagg smiled sombrely to himself in the darkness, as the little Dutchman turned to the right to cut across the hills to his own road, and big white Skater kept on, to take advantage of the Seco Trail for a few miles more to the north. Then, at a point where Seco Trail took a sudden swing east, Stagg swung Skater west and slightly north, in a due line for the Crazy L. Before he had gone much farther, the full moon was above the horizon, every star was glowing, paling the night sky, so that travel was simple by the clear night light, and Stagg was lost in the rather lonely beauty of the open range in its solitude.

Before Stagg was more than halfway to the Crazy L, Kurt Quillan rode across the triangular corner of the Cross-Bar which thrust to the south, and onto the L-Over-S. In the clear moonlight he passed close to several head of cattle, and on two of them he could see against white patches of hide the dark outline of Lem Strickland's brand, LS. Just a straight L above a straight S. In a clump of oaks he tied the Arabian deep in shade, and went ahead cautiously afoot.

The house, the good-sized frame house Lem

had built for Mrs. Strickland, was dark. There was no sign of life about it. Quillan hazarded that perhaps both Mrs. Strickland and her hired girl were long since in bed asleep. He slipped past the house, and on toward the other buildings beyond it. There was no light in the bunk house either, and Quillan moved with the soundlessness and seeming lack of substance that there is in a shifting shadow, and abruptly ceased moving as he saw the dim glow of a lantern in the saddle room at the end of the barn.

Somebody was up, but this was a strange time of night to be mending harness, or repairing gear in the saddle room. Kurt's tall figure flowed like a shifting shadow again, in that soundless motion; and suddenly darted, as a shadow seems to leap crazily, when a light that causes it is lifted abruptly from one place to another, and came to rest again at the end of the barn, beside the one small window let into the outer wall of the saddle room.

Quillan was tall enough to peer into the lower end of the little dingy pane merely by standing to his height, and he saw within, in the steady glow of a lantern hung on the wall, two of the L-Over-S men bent over something on which one of them was working busily. There was about them an air of intense concentration as if the object before them was something of great importance, not to be handled carelessly or in a haste which made for shoddy workmanship. One of the men was wielding a heavy needle strung on a long stout thread, the other was holding in place a stout piece of finely tanned leather.

Then the man with the needle moved, and Quillan saw what lay on the upended box between them. It was a tiny trunk, such as a woman might use for trinkets, fashioned of cedar; the open lid showed the clear, red-grained colour of the wood. The two men had covered the trunk with fine leather, banded it by hand with copper, and were just adding the finishing tightening draw to the leather at one end.

The man who was holding the end of the strip of leather nodded admiringly. He spoke, and his lowered voice came faintly but intelligibly to Quillan's ears.

"She's sure to like this, Rocky. That was a swell idea you had. Damned if I'd know just what to fix for a woman if you hadn't suggested this. You done a swell job on the box itself, even."

Rocky pursed his lips in absorption, but made no answer, and Quillan slipped back from the window and moved along the side of the barn toward the half-open door a few yards away, wondering what was the meaning of that scene. Rocky had no girl, and the only woman on the ranch that the boys would be making gifts to please was Mrs. Strickland; and usually they didn't go to that much trouble about anything of the sort unless somebody's birthday, or a similar holiday, loomed in the offing.

Kurt entered the half-open barn door and passed through the barn without a sound, and like the shadow he resembled came to a stop in the open door of the saddle room, both guns drawn. And the man holding the strip of leather felt somehow that pent incandescent force, and looked up, and stiffened, and dropped the piece of leather.

"What the devil's the matter with you?" demanded Rocky crossly.

The other man wet his lips. "Look—behind you."

Rocky frowned, hesitated a moment, and turned slowly enough, but when he saw who was there he jabbed the heavy needle into the ball of his thumb, and didn't feel it.

"What—what do you want here, Kurt?" He tried to sound casual, but his eyes were fixed in fascination on the right-hand gun Kurt held, and his voice echoed the expression quivering in them. "What do you want!"

"Don't be a damned fool, Rocky." Quillan's gaze was like the gleam of fine blue glass under a jeweller's loupe, and you couldn't say it was threatening, you couldn't say it was cold, but you'd have felt a nameless certainty that somewhere behind it burned mockery, and bitterness, and a species of contempt. "I'm not going to shoot anybody. I just want to make certain that somebody doesn't shoot me. I want to speak to Coke. Will you go tell him to come out for a minute?"

"He isn't here." Rocky's sensitive fingers moved slightly upon the tiny trunk. "He left Arroyo on the ten-o'clock train last night."

Something emanated from Quillan like an escaped charge of that leaping force, yet nothing about him moved. "Where did he go?"

"Why, he just went to Madder Junction for a few days. He'll be back next week, he said. What do you want of Coke?"

Quillan ignored the question. "Then I want to see Mrs. Strickland. Sorry to get her up this time of night, but it's important."

Rocky shook his head, and his first startled fear had been bolstered by a grim resentment. "I wouldn't call her for you even if she was here, which she ain't. She went with Coke."

There could be no doubt of that leap of triumph in Quillan's clean blue eyes, but his voice remained subdued, even. "What did they go for, and why did they go together?"

Rocky's resentment flared. "I can't see that it's any of your damned business. But"—his hand caressed the tiny trunk—"this is a wedding present. They went to be married. I know it's kind of soon after Lem being gone, but Coke's been in love with her ever since he was knee-high. She turned him down for Lem, which didn't pan out so good, and Coke's been waiting for her ever since. Looks to me like he kind of deserved to get her at last. And now that you know all about it, will you kindly get out of here and stay out? The next time you show your face, you won't take anybody off guard this way, and you won't live long enough to know what a low-down skunk we think you are."

Quillan's wide shoulders moved in an indescribably contemptuous shrug. "If shooting the man who killed my mother is being a skunk, I'm it. I was a fool for letting him live so long."

"Killed your mother?" Rocky stared. "You're crazy! Lem wouldn't have killed a chicken! And nothing you can ever do could be big enough to make any man on this range wipe out the fact that you deliberately shot him down. You can go skulking around behind the protection of them guns just so long as nobody manages to get the drop on you, and no longer. You'll pay for Lem so damned fast you'll never know what hit you, the first time you get a little careless."

There was nothing about Quillan to evidence that he had heard a word of Rocky's angry denouncing threat, unless it was that the aura of mocking contempt radiating from him seemed to grow in tensity. "Lem killed my mother Rocky. That isn't all he did. As long as he lived he kept me from knowing that my mother owned this ranch, and that she had left it to me as my legal inheritance when I should come of age. And I'm going to bring proof of it, and take what belongs to me. You might as well know it now, and get used to the idea."

Rocky's anger flamed to fury. Where some men flushed with ire, Rocky paled, and now he went quite white. "Get out of here! You won't live long enough to try any such damned underhanded trick. Lem owned this ranch before your mother was killed. Before she was ever heard of around here. I know the whole story. Mrs. Strickland married him for a home, and Coke was the kind of poor duffer that never can seem to get ahead; a lot of women have made that fool mistake and lived to be sorry for it.

"Lem never loved her; he married her to have a wife to bring you up, and she soon found it out, but she stuck to her bargain, because she's the right sort, and she gave a good many years to the thankless job of trying to make a man out of you. She's earned this ranch, and she's earned Coke, and if they want to get married the day Lem was buried that's their business. Now get out of here, because I can't stand the sight of you! Get!"

He blinked his eyes and cut himself short. Quillan had gone from sight so soundlessly and so quickly that one instant Rocky was glaring furiously into the cold-blue eyes, and the next half of the same instant he was staring into empty darkness. He started to leap toward the door, and the other cowboy flung himself in front of him and laid a hand on his chest and pushed him back.

"Take it easy, Rocky! Don't lam out there and get yourself shot! You can't reach the bunk house and get your gun in time to do anything. It's too dangerous trying to round him up in the night anyway. If somebody don't get him in the next day or two, we'll get up a posse that will make Pete Gulick's look like a hen party, and we'll put an end to this damn foolishness. But I'm not going to let you walk right into it like that."

"I guess you're right." Rocky turned back to the upended box. "I've got to get this done and shined up good anyhow. But of all the fool things to say, that Lem killed his mother, and that his mother owned this ranch. He sure has big ideas, anyway, don't he?"

Kurt, just outside the small window let into the saddle-room wall, smiled thinly and was gone into the shining night, along the trees in the yard, like one shadow melting into another. As he reached the copse where he had left the Arabian, mounted the horse and rode him away at a quiet walk, he was still smiling. He had at least started the ball rolling downhill. How rapidly events were building the proof of what he and the others had discussed at the doctor's house; he had need to get to Stagg, to tell him, and to pursue the way he had taken with all possible

173

speed. The instant Coke and Mrs. Strickland returned, Rocky would tell them what had been said there in the saddle room, and all that verged toward the clearing of the tangled situation must be ready to break over their heads before they could move to underhanded defence.

Once well down the road leading away from the L-Over-S, Quillan gave the Arabian his head, and swung north across the triangular lower corner of the Cross-Bar. He felt a fleeting sense of amusement that he could have even suggested Frank Cross as a possible suspect, as being the man masquerading in clothes like Louie's and behind a bandanna to hide his face. Why should Frank Cross want to scheme against him, or have any covetous eye on the L-Over-S?

Frank had a good ranch of his own; it was smaller than the L-Over-S, the buildings were poorer, his cattle fewer, but it was still a good ranch. Nothing about the thought was compatible with the deed. Not in a thousand years could it be Frank Cross. But little proof was needed now, to bring Coke Laughlin into the open, and lay bare the entire sinister scheme.

Quillan crossed the railroad and advanced into the hilly stretch that intervened between the Cross Bar and the branch road that ended in Seco Trail to the north. His ordered and precisely functioning intelligence was sorting all the sections of the tangle geometrically into form, each fact in its certain position, each suspicion in its probable situation, and he came inevitably to the jagged piece none had noticed yet, and he wondered how they all could have been so blind.

Cottrelle had disappeared, Barnes was probably following the same fate right now. Neither of them would ever be seen alive again. Some man who feared some revelation that could transpire through either or both of them had simply met them there in that area into which they had vanished, and put them out of the way. Some man to whom the uncovering of the twisted pattern of menace that had followed him, Kurt Quillan, would be disaster. Some man who wore red angora chaps and a tan hat and wanted to leave Lispy Louie to pay the bill. And who in that territory could answer to all of those designations? Lon Ivey. Lon, who had quarrelled with Lem, and who was probably as poor a specimen of humanity as Lem had ever been.

And Quillan rode on into the open range, north-west toward the Crazy L, wondering if Stagg had reached there yet, and whether he had unearthed anything concerning Lispy Louie or Lon Ivey.

Stagg was at that time almost to the south line of the Crazy L. He glanced across to the left and north-west, and saw that there was a light in Ivey's house. He decided abruptly that he might as well speak to Lon immediately, since he would probably be there in the house alone, and there would be no small annoyance of getting him aside from any of the ranch hands.

Stagg swerved Skater to the left, and approached the big stone house looming black in the moonlight, under the three towering oak trees that were such a rich green background for the grey stone in the day. The light showing was in the rear of the house, in the kitchen most likely, Stagg judged, though he had never been this close to Ivey's house before and couldn't be certain.

He halted Skater beside the pillared back porch, and went up the steps lightly. But the man inside had heard the faint sound of his footsteps, and swung open the door. The bright light of the coal oil mantle lamp revealed the man in the kitchen with sharp clarity; a middle-sized man, with greying brown hair, a broad, heavy face, with an enormous jutting jaw, and high cheek bones. He had a flour sack tied about his stout middle, and he held a long cooking fork in one hand.

"Evenin'!" he greeted Stagg heartily. "Looking for somebody?"

Stagg's slow smile enveloped him. "You don't remember me, do you? I'm sure I've seen you in Seco Springs several times. You're José Sanchez, aren't you?"

Sanchez's thick brows lifted, and recognition brightened his heavy face. "Yes, of course. Excuse me! I know you now. You're Bill Stagg, from the Circle G! Come right in. I was just getting dinner for the boss. Were you wanting to see Ivey?"

Stagg's gaze lingered, half fascinated, on the enormous out-thrust jaw, as he stepped inside and closed the door. "Why, yes. I was. But I certainly didn't mean to interrupt his supper. I had no idea he'd be eating so late."

"Oh, that's all right." Sanchez waved a hand toward a near-by chair. "Sit down, Stagg. The boss isn't here, but he'll be along pretty quick. There isn't a soul home right now but me. The cook has to be always on the job."

He grinned, and his jaw seemed to increase in size, as his lips backed away from it to show fine even teeth that were chalk white. "Five of the boys went into Seco Springs this afternoon to cash their pay checks and have a little fun. Ivey and the other four left about daylight to trail a herd of whitefaces, that Pat Ryan bought, over to the Seven Up. I went with 'em as far as Seco Trail, and then turned back to have dinner ready for the boss when he came home. He'll be here before long, and he'll be hungry as a wolf with pups. Have a slice of roast beef and a baked spud while you're waiting?"

"No, thanks, José. I don't believe I'm hungry. By gad, this is a fine house, isn't it?"

"Just about the best on the range," José answered warmly and proudly. "It's old, but it's one of the kind that gets better with age. The boss built it for his wife. He was married once, you know. But she died. It's kind of sad, and we don't never talk about it. Don't ever repeat that. I sort of said it without thinking. Ivey never could think of putting any other woman in her place. He don't ever mention her any more, but if you know him you can see pretty plain that after she died he didn't have much to live for. You know the boss well?"

"No, I don't, José. Not much more than to speak to sociably. But we've been having some trouble down our way, and I wanted to ask him if he could tell me anything to help straighten it out."

"Oh, you mean about Kurt Quillan?" José eyed the beef roast critically, slipped it back into the oven, and turned to lay the cooking fork on the drain board. "Yeah, us boys heard about it; about you taking him for a loop. He getting hard to handle? I guess he'd—huh! Sounds like the boss and the other boys coming now. Nope—only one horse."

He hurried to the door and threw it wide, peered out into the night, and called loudly: "That you, boss? Where's the rest of the boys?"

A voice answered from the night. "Sho' it's me, José. The rest of the boys cut down to Seco Springs. As hankerin' for a good time as a passell of kids, so I told 'em they could go. Reckon you'n me'll be eatin' alone to-night."

"Nope!" José returned, with the delighted

178

heartiness of a man relaying very good news. "We got company. Hurry in, boss."

"Comp'ny!" said the voice outside. "Waal, I swan to goodness! I'll be there as soon as I can put this nag up."

José closed the door and turned to beam on Stagg with a grin that looked cavernous behind that enormous jaw. "We don't get much company away off up here, with the whole open range between us and the other ranchers, and both towns far away. Nobody near but Lispy Louie, and he wouldn't be fit company for a sick coyote." José chuckled at his own heavy wit, as he bustled to the stove to take up the steaming dinner waiting for Lon Ivey. He continued to gabble garrulously, till the stamp of feet ascended the back stairs, and the door swung back, and Ivey stepped into the room.

Stagg's still black eyes turned to him in a penetrating scrutiny. Ivey was little and thin, the equal of Lispy Louie in size almost to a pound. His hair was black above his smooth-shaven, sun-tanned face, and his black brows and lashes made his hazel eyes, a much lighter hazel than Pete Gulick's, look like thin-veined moss agate. His lean face lighted as he took off his hat and welcomed Stagg.

"So you're the comp'ny! Waal, I swan, now, Bill. You couldn't have come at a better time. I'm always hankerin' for comp'ny, and sho' get little enough of it, and I been ridin' all day since dawn, shaggin' that pesky herd all the way to the Seven Up, gettin' back almighty hungry and saddle weary. Sho' am glad to see you, Bill. Set in. Set in! You can't refuse to eat with me. José's a real fine cook. Sorry to keep you waitin' so long, José. I come as fast as I could."

"Oh, that's all right, boss." José's heavy face was still beaming, as he heaved laden dishes upon the table, and Ivey sat down at the board, and Stagg accepted a seat opposite him rather than argue about it.

José paused by Ivey with a deprecating gesture. "I'm not hungry, boss. So I think I'll amble on out to the bunk-house. Bill said he wanted to talk to you, and you don't want no third man sitting around listening in. Everything's on the table but the pie, and it's in the cooler. Anything else you want of me before I go?"

"Waal, no; no, I reckon not, José. Trot yourself along. I know, you're hankerin' to get at that whittlin' of yours. You've done enough work for one day, anyhow." Ivey passed the roast to Stagg, as José laid aside his flour-sack apron and his heavy feet thumped noisily from the room. "Take a good helping, Bill. I always look forward to gettin' home to one of Jose's meals. Now, what was it you wanted to see me about, Bill?"

CHAPTER XI

LON TELLS A STORY

ANY other man but Bill Stagg, only a little less determined on the dogged pursuit of the truth than that huge man, might have been so disarmed by Ivey's delight in his advent, by Ivey's unsuspecting hospitality, that he would have hesitated to pursue the intent to elicit information which had motivated him in coming. Not Bill Stagg. Neither Lon Ivey nor any other man could evade his slow but remorseless drive toward the hidden truth, either by cunning evasion or by artless and naïve innocence. Stagg accepted a slice of savoury browned beef, as he answered Ivey's question.

"I wanted to see you about several things, Lon; Kurt Quillan, for one, and Lem, and Warren Cottrelle, for others."

"Sho', now; is that so?" Ivey split a bulging baked potato, and poked a large lump of butter into its puffing white insides. "Better have some of this butter, Bill. José insists on keeping milch cows and having cream and butter. Waal, now, Bill, I reckon I can tell you more about Kurt and Lem than anybody else, but I'm bound to tucker out when it comes to Cottrelle. The man's a plumb stranger to me, and I hope he's left the neighbourhood for good. I swan, I'm gettin' tired of the sound of his name! Just what was it you wanted to know, Bill?"

Stagg thoughtfully stirred the smoking brown gravy as he began to ladle it onto his plate. "Did Owen Barnes stop here in the last day or so, Lon? Or haven't you ever heard of him either?"

"Owen Barnes!" Ivey's hands went still in their task of buttering the baked potato. His mild, light-hazel eyes gleamed a little, as if the light of excitement had wakened in their moss-agate irises. "I swan, Bill. That was the name of my poor wife's brother. The last letter she ever writ was to him. I mailed it myself when I was on a business trip to Madder Junction, many a year ago. You can't mean that Owen Barnes, I take it?"

"If your wife was Bess Quillan, that's the Barnes I mean." Stagg's gaze held on Ivey's face, quiet and restrained, but a little puzzled, and wondering. He had not expected to meet such unhesitating frankness in Lon Ivey. "He came into Arroyo a few days ago looking for you, and Mordan directed him here."

"My gonnies, I wonder if he could have missed the way? I never did know him personal, but Bess—yes, she was Bess Barnes Quillan—she talked of him a lot. Sho' did. She thought a heap of him. I woulda writ to him after she died, but I never thought to take that address from that letter, and I—I—Waal, I wasn't expectin' her to die, Bill. It come awful sudden. You been here on this range quite a spell, seems like. Maybe you might have heard the story. It's pretty sad."

Only Stagg's unalterable purpose drove him on then, but he told himself that he had loved Bess Quillan, too; he had an unquestionable right to prevent harsh eventualities that would have meant heartbreak to her had she lived. He said quietly:

"Yes, I have heard it, Lon. I didn't know she was your wife. I didn't know she had ever been on this part of the range at all. I don't believe any one else knows it. No one knows anything save that Lem found her dead in Lobo Pass, buried her and brought up Kurt. I—I hate to ask this, Lon; to probe into anything that can hurt. But, have you any idea who killed her?"

The mild hazel eyes darkened, as fine-grained moss-agate would darken were it suddenly sunken under inches of water. Ivey's sun-tanned face set and he stared hard at Stagg for an instant. Then he answered slowly: "I don't know what you're trying to get at, Bill, but I'm no mind to hinder you by keeping my mouth shut in the wrong place; only this is between you and me, understand, and it's never to go one man farther.

"He's dead now, and it might not seem to matter, but I don't want it to get out that I've got a flippety tongue. Lem Strickland killed her, Bill. I'm the only man that ever knew that, and

I've had sense enough to keep it. Though it wasn't easy to go on through the years, seeing him live on, and aching to choke him to death every time I looked on him."

"How do you know he killed her?" Stagg felt something hushed and waiting within him, reaching toward the heart of that old mystery. "How could you know it without being there, Lon?"

Ivey passed his hand over his eyes, and when he lowered it the hand was shaking. "I was there. Bess and me hadn't been married more'n about a month, Bill. I swan, that was the happiest month I ever see. Then she got a hankerin' for some new duds, like women will, and they wa'n't much she could buy at Seco Springs, as you can imagine. So we agreed to take Kurt and go to Madder Junction, and make a kind of festivatin' day of it. We started early mornin', and come nigh dark we was gettin' on to Lobo Pass. And right there Lem Strickland jumped onto me. I swan, Bill, that was the most suddenest and unexpected thing!

"He started firin' at both of us, and I went fair blind when I saw Bess reel out of the saddle, and poor little Kurt fall on top of her. By that time I'd got my gun out, and by gonnies, I went for him. But I'm slow. He jerked his horse around and run, down Seco Trail. I stopped to look at my Bess, and she was dead, and I didn't want nothin' right then but to kill him. I got onto my horse and took after him. And hang my luck, Bill, but some other damn fool come ridin' through the pass, and I guess he musta thought it was me shot Bess, and he took after me, shootin'.

"He got me, too." Ivey sighed, and gripped his hands together, and his tanned face was bleached and lined. "Knocked me flat on my horse's back. I kept going as far as I could, and he turned back, and I couldn't keep saddle no longer. I fell out of the saddle to the ground, and my horse stopped, and I plumb fainted. He got me in the side, pretty bad, and I lay there near all night before I could get on my horse again. I rode back to the pass, but Bess and Kurt was gone, and I went home. I like to have died. I didn't find out till weeks later what had become of Bess and Kurt. And there wa'n't nothin' I could do then."

"By gad, you should have killed him!" Stagg's black eyes were hot with indignation. "Whatever stopped you? Why did he ever attack you in such a manner?"

"Do I have to tell you that, too?" Ivey asked starkly.

"I was the other damned fool in the pass," said Stagg. "I did think it was you who had shot Bess. I'm sorry for the suffering I caused you, but I wish you'd tell me what I just asked, Lon."

"Waal, I reckon there's no reason I shouldn't, but it kind of tears me up inside to think of it.

You see, the beginning of it was that Bess come here in the first place to marry Lem. She met him when he was in Chicago with a beef herd. She was living in Chicago, and her husband had died and left her with Kurt, and she was plumb lonesome, and Lem he kind of took to her, and asked her would she come out here and marry him and live on his ranch. She didn't hanker for him none. She told me that.

"But she was tired of the city, and she had that idea about it being a better place to raise the little fella in the country. That's a true idea, too. So she told Lem she'd come out in a few weeks and marry him, and she'd write him when to look for her. She did write him, but they was a washout on the railroad, and her letter got delayed. She got to Madder Junction the day before her letter got to Seco Springs. So, of course, when she got off at Madder Junction there wa'n't nobody there to meet her, and she was sort of worried.

"I happened to be there with a herd I'd took in to ship, and the station agent told her I could see her to the L-Over-S, and I said I'd be plumb delighted to do such a pleasantry. I'd never heard of her, and I didn't know what she was going to Lem's ranch for, but that wa'n't none of my business. I always took along a couple of extra saddle horses, so I had a mount for her, and we got organized and started back together. We had to go slow, being as we didn't want to make it no tiring travel for her and the little boy, so I sent my two cowhands on ahead.

"As her and me rode along I got pretty struck with her, she was an awful pretty-appearin' woman, and she got friendly, and told me she had come here to marry Lem, and now she'd got this far she was frightened, and she didn't want to go through with it, but she didn't know what else she could do. I couldn't help feelin' mighty sorry for her, and I sho' was took with her. I swan, Bill, she was the prettiest thing I ever see.

"It didn't seem right nohow for her to have to marry Lem Strickland or any other man if she wa'n't hankerin' for it. So I told her I had a pretty fair ranch myself, and if she cared to do it, she could come home with me, she and the boy, and she could just keep house for me, and think it over, and see what she wanted to do. I swan, Bill, she was so tickled that it was plumb touchin' the way she took me up so quick. Seemed like we couldn't get to the ranch quick enough to please her.

"And, waal, she wa'n't here more'n a month till she decided that this was the place she wanted to stay, so she writ Lem a letter explainin' where she was and how she felt, and I left it for him at Seco Springs. I kind of wanted to have the weddin' right away, but she wanted us to have a nice house first, and I wa'n't minded to hinder no woman's hankerin's so long as they was reasonable. So we got the stuff up and had this house built, then we went to Madder Junction and was married. And a month later she was killed. If I could have shot Lem that night I'd have done it.

"But after I got well from the bullet I took, I knew I couldn't do it and raise a lot of scandal about her name. Her bein' killed that way was bad enough. There wa'n't no sense in makin' it worse. I went to see Lem, after I heard the story he'd give out, and faced him with it, and plumb demanded Bess's boy as was my right. Lem was terrible. He was eat up by the jealousy that had made him kill her and try to kill me. He said he'd had a right to Bess afore me and he was going to keep Kurt, and if I ever bothered him any, he'd tell all about how I took Bess away from him, and he'd make it look pretty nasty, her living here in my house so long before we was married.

"My hands was sort of tied, Bill. For her sake, there wa'n't a thing I could do. Lem was red in the face he was so mad, and he went on to say I'd better never let it be known that I'd had anything to do with Bess at all. Nobody had heard yet about her comin' in and bein' at my place, and he didn't want anybody ever to know. Just let it lie as it was, or he'd make such a scandal about Bess I'd wish I hadn't never seen the light of day. So I had to go away and leave Kurt there, and keep all my sorrow and bitterness in my own heart, but I told Lem if he ever so much as mistreated Kurt, I'd kill him, let come what may.

"And that's the whole story, Bill. I don't see what you can do about it for Kurt's sake now. The poor boy's gone plumb to the dogs, and I'm sho' prayerful glad his poor mother never lived to see it."

Stagg's breath drew in, so sharp and hard that it hurt his lungs by its pressure. "Is there any possibility, Lon, that Kurt could have any right to the L-Over-S?"

"None as I know of, Bill. By rights, Lem should have arranged to leave the boy somethin', but I don't reckon he did. Lem was a hard man, and though he come to his death in a hard way, seems like there's a kind of Almighty justice in it."

"Suppose I'd tell you that I know there is a deed in existence, Lon, which shows that Bess bought the L-Over-S about three months before she married you. That I've seen it."

"Waal, I swan, Bill. I wouldn't be wantin' to doubt your word, none, but I don't see how that could have took place. Bess had a little money that come to her when her first husband died, but she spent most of it on this house, wantin' a real nice place, like women get a yearnin' for; I'd put all my ready cash into a new strain of whitefaces then, and she wanted to do it. And I don't see how she could have bought any ranch without my knowin' it, Bill, or why of all places she'd took a fancy to the L-Over-S. This is a sight better ranch than the L-Over-S could ever be, more land, better water, better buildin's. Better everything."

"Well, maybe somebody's been fooling me, Lon." Stagg pushed back his chair from the table. "I wonder if you'd mind letting me see your wedding certificate, Lon? If that sounds like a queer request, I'm sorry. But I'd just like to see it."

"Sho', Bill! That's too bad, now. I'd be glad to let you see it if I could, but Bess used to take care of that weddin' paper, and after she was killed I never could find it again. I don't know what she done with it. I guess you think I'm real low for shootin' at Kurt. But you know how he'd been goin' around killin', and I thought when I come up to face him there I was done for. I didn't go to hurt him bad, I just wanted to stop him. Then I see he didn't have no gun. I've been feelin' real remorseful about that, but when you see him again you might tell him. I don't want Bess's boy to have no hard feelin's toward me."

"I'll tell him." Stagg rose from his chair. "I'm afraid I've been thinking pretty harsh things of you, Lon. I'm sorry. It's too bad to wrong any other man even in your thoughts. Which reminds me that you've been thinking wrong of Louie, Lon. It wasn't Louie running brands on your cattle. It was some pretty bad jasper dressing in clothes like Louie's, up to all kinds of dirty work, and trying to lay the blame on Louie."

190

"Waal, by gonnies, Bill! You tell Louie I'm regretful about that. I'd like to get my fingers on that fella. You got any idea who he is?"

"No, not yet, Lon. But I think maybe he could tell us what become of Cottrelle, and if Barnes hasn't come here yet, he isn't going to come, and I suspect the little devil in red chaps could tell us something about that, too. Don't let it worry you, Lon. If we decide to get up another posse and clean this range to find him, can we count on you?"

Ivey followed Stagg to the door, his sun-tanned face alive with excitement and eagerness. "I swear you can, Bill. Me and all my boys. They'll be home come evenin' to-morrow, and all you got to do is give us word. I get almighty lonesome for comp'ny. Come callin' again when you got time to spare, Bill."

"I will, Lon." Stagg's deep voice warmed, as he looked back at the solitary little man framed in the light of the bright lamp.

"Dog-gone it," the huge man muttered to himself as he walked toward the waiting Skater. "There are even things he don't know. Now why in thunder didn't I ask him what he and Lem were quarrelling about that night? Well, I won't go back and bother him any more to-night. I'll ask him the next time I see him. I'd better move along or I won't reach Louie's before midnight."

CHAPTER XII
DEAD MEN TELL TOO LITTLE

WHEN Stagg rode up to the rough little cabin where Lispy Louie lived, there was no light, but there was sound. There was the strange and startling sound of a man muttering to himself, in short, ugly gasps. Stagg stood for a moment in stillness in the small yard, then went softly forward, listening, before he could believe that his hearing was correct. Some one inside was muttering, choking, sickeningly, in utter terror.

Two steps of Stagg's long legs took him up the three low stairs and across the narrow porch. He flung the door open and called out:

"Louie!"

The hideous chattering choked off, and then began again, surprised to a kind of ghastly shudder-ing moan. Stagg struck a match, and held it high. Louie lay face down half on the floor and half on the bunk his head hidden in his arms, his entire body racked with spasmodic quivers that started at his feet and crawled upward.

Stagg lighted the small lamp on the table and threw the match onto the old iron stove, then bent, seized Louie's shoulder and pulled him upright. The little man's greasy face was bloated and bleached to a pasty pallor, he had literally

192

worried himself sick. His cocked eye looked like a dead eye, and his good eye was bloodshot and swollen. He swayed under Stagg's hand, barely able to keep his feet.

"Louie!" Stagg's deep tones rumbled their dismay, his black eyes widened in consternation. "For the love of Pete, man! What's happened?"

"I—I can't te-tell you!" Louie's voice sounded as a mere hoarse gasp. "I—don't—dare. But you—you told me—to look around—Oh, go away, Bill. Pleathe—go away! I can't tell you— nothin'!"

Stagg lowered him gently to the foot of the bed, and stood looking down at him. Louie sat where Stagg had placed him, huddled in misery, still shaken by his gasps of terror. Stagg studied him for a moment in silence; no amount of compassion or sympathy would touch a man in Louie's state, but striving harshly to force him to control might work. Stagg had seen it work before. His level organ voice hardened:

"Louie, you've come across something important. Straighten up here and tell me what it is or I'll choke it out of you."

Louie's head jerked up, the cocked eye rolled, and the other eye came to life. That good eye was lighted by a dogged defiance. "Go ahead and choke! You can kill me, but I won't tell. You'd kill a man quick and clean, anyhow. You wouldn't—torture him!"

"Torture!" Stagg involuntarily backed a pace. "Good gosh, Louie, what is this? You've run onto plenty to make you as afraid as all that. You'll have to tell, Louie! You might as well get started. I won't let up on you till you tell!"

"I won't!" Louie fairly babbled, and his pasty face worked. He was crawling with fear of something too unspeakable, too frightful, to be considered with any degree of equanimity. "I like you, Bill. You're a thwell guy. You're the only guy that ever liked me. But you wouldn't like me any more if you found out. You wouldn't believe me any more. I got to go away quick, before thomebody elthe findth out."

"Listen, Louie: get a grip on yourself, will you?" Stagg sat down on the edge of the bunk beside Lispy, and turned the little man about to face him. "I know somebody is trying to frame you, trying to make you the goat for something or other. You can tell me anything, and I'll stick with you and protect you. Now, out with it."

"No—no!" Louie panted. "No! You couldn't protect me, not even you, if anybody elthe found it out. I won't tell. Not for you nor nobody elthe."

Stagg knew when he was stopped. Louie was demoralized beyond all consideration of anything save the fear that had shrivelled his soul to an insensate mass of misery. Were he allowed to regain control of himself, to sleep off his exhaustion, there might be some hope of persuading him that in his case silence was far from golden. Stagg reached out a hand and gripped Louie's thin, shrinking shoulder.

"All right, Louie. I won't badger you. It's getting late, anyhow. Lie down there and see if you can't sleep. I'm here now, and nobody's going to bother you. I promise you that, so you should be able to relax and forget your troubles for a while. Lie down, you poor devil. We're still working together, Louie."

He shoved the little man bodily back onto the bed, and Louie's eyes closed, and his breath rasped through his throat in catches. In spite of his terror, Stagg's presence, the controlled psychological influence of Stagg's steady mind, the physical bulwark of Stagg's huge, powerful body, had an effect against which Louie's frantic fear was stilled, under which Louie's helpless panic subsided. Within fifteen minutes the little man was sleeping the sleep of exhaustion, snoring loudly.

Stagg rose from the edge of the bed and looked around the cabin. He could see nothing to indicate the cause for Louie's collapse. He went outside and looked around, but the moonlight was waning, and nothing unusual presented itself. He returned to the cabin, blew the lamp out, and stretched on the one wide bunk between Louie and the wall. He went to sleep almost as quickly as Louie, and he awoke in the early morning, conscious that he had been aroused by Louie's slipping off the bed.

Louie was just tiptoeing out the door.

Stagg lay motionless till he heard Louie leave the porch, then he rolled off the bunk, fully dressed as he had lain all night, and stepped to the small window beside the door. Louie was going rapidly toward his small barn. Stagg waited till the little man was out of sight inside the barn, then he followed. He walked stealthily up to the little structure, and peered through a crack between two of the boards that formed the side walls. A minute passed before his sight located Louie in the half darkness of the small barn's interior, and what Stagg saw would have made a less-controlled man gasp.

Louie was on his knees, digging a hole in the dirt floor of his barn. Beside him lay some small object wrapped in an old scrap of newspaper. Patiently, he was going to bury the object in the hole. For an instant Stagg debated whether to walk in on him, or wait till he had opportunity to ascertain what the object was before facing Louie with it.

He decided to wait. He stood watching till he saw Louie lower the object into the hole and start to replace the dirt over it. Then Stagg returned to the house and opened the door. Without entering the house, he closed the door with a bang, stamped across the porch, and called loudly:

"Louie! Oh, Louie! Time for breakfast."

Almost immediately Louie came hurrying out of the barn, and even at that distance there was about him a furtive and half-guilty air. But he had got himself in hand again, and he answered promptly:

"Here I am, Bill. I wath hopin' you'd thleep a little longer. I'll be right in and get thome breakfatht. Could you eat fricatheed chicken thith early in the mornin'? I got thome thwell fricathee that I cooked yethderday before—" He cut off his words with a quick gasp, and Stagg knew what he would have said, that he had cooked the chicken before his terror had come upon him.

But the big man ignored it. He said good-naturedly: "I can eat fricasseed chicken any time. Come on and let's see the colour of it."

Now, a strange little byplay occurred by that small rude barn. It was a very open-air barn as you might say, the boards of the walls had shrunk and split in various places under the assault of the elements, so that the faintest breeze blew through the cracks in the summer, and the snow drifted through them in the winter, and on any side of the barn a man could peer into it without having to look very far for an interstice to accommodate his eye.

Beyond the barn were two small groves and numerous scattered trees. Louie liked trees, and he had left them standing all around.

As Stagg had stepped out of the house to follow Louie, Kurt Quillan, after riding steadily across the open range all night, had approached from the east, behind the trees. The trees hid him and the brown Arabian, but between them he could see Stagg striding toward the barn. He dropped the Arabian's reins over a limb and slipped ahead between the trees, intending to intercept Stagg. Then he saw Stagg round the end of the barn, put his face to a crack and peer inside.

This action did not exactly arouse Kurt's curiosity. It did inform him instantly that something worth investigating was occurring in the barn. He slipped through the nearby trees, with that walk which one would have sworn could have made no sound on any substance, and stepped up to the other end of the barn, and found himself a crack between two split boards, and peered in also. He watched Louie bury the object. He heard Stagg's voice call from the porch, and guessed what Stagg's further action and ruse had been.

He saw Louie hurry out of the barn, and he remained where he was, listening to the short conversation between Stagg and Lispy Louie. Then when he heard Louie start toward the house, he moved to the corner of the barn and peered past it. The instant Stagg and Louie stepped into the house and the door closed, Quillan flashed around the corner and into the barn.

The spot where Louie had been burying the small object wrapped in newspaper was instantly discernible, a darker damp patch in the hard-packed earth. Quillan picked up the shovel Louie had laid aside and uncovered the small package with a few effortless heaves of the loosened dirt. He dropped the shovel, and stepped to the barn window to unwrap the small hard thing the paper covered.

It was a watch, a large silver watch of an ancient type. Some one had carried it for many years and cherished it. The case was worn so smooth that the faintest of broken lines and curves were all that remained of the original chasing. Nothing was on the outside of the case to reveal who the owner might have been.

Kurt pried back the hunting case from over the face. Nothing was there, either, but the time-yellowed dial, the numerals worked in blue enamel. Kurt snapped shut the case over the face and pried open the back cover that protected the works.

His cold gaze held, still and emotionless, on the words engraved in the gleaming silver of the reverse surface of the back.

To
WARREN G. COTTRELLE
in appreciation
of
his work in the
Avermund case
from
B. D. AVERMUND, SR.

Kurt closed the watch, simply by closing the hand that held it, and walked with that lithe light tread out of the barn, and again slipped around the corner of the small structure out of sight from the house. By moving from building to tree, and from tree to shed and shed to grove, he reached the house without exposing himself to view of anyone who might happen to emerge from the rear cabin door. He ceased to move, in that queer, effortless pause, beside the window nearest the old iron stove.

Louie was hurrying his fire, and testing his fricassee chicken, and measuring coffee, with his back toward Stagg. Kurt could hear Stagg's organ bass saying gently:

"Whatever it was you ran onto yesterday, Louie, you have to tell me in self-defence. You have to do it to save your own hide."

But Louie had grown certain that Stagg would never adopt any harsh measures to force his tongue, and Louie had no intention of being in that part of the country by the time night fell again. He carried a dish of chicken to the table, and motioned to the place he had set for Stagg. "Draw up and eat, old-timer. I gueth I don't know nothin' to tell, Bill." He sat down opposite Stagg.

Neither of them heard a step on the porch. Neither of them heard the door latch or unlatch. A light grew and died as the door opened and closed, and they both looked up, and Kurt was standing there.

He moved toward them, and Louie stared at him, and wet his lips, and Stagg sat as if even his blood had gone still, waiting. Kurt reached the table. He extended his right hand, its long brown fingers closed, and laid the loosely clenched fist upon the table top between Stagg and Louie, the back of the hand down. Louie's one good eye, still strained and bloodshot, followed the motion of that closed hand in sickening fascination.

Kurt opened his hand, by simply relaxing the fingers and letting them fall back. In the palm of his hand lay Cottrelle's watch. "Once the property of Warren G. Cottrelle," said Kurt's voice, almost like a deadly sound of caress, "buried in your barn. Talk, Louie."

Louie looked as if someone had drained all the blood out of his body and melted the bones in his flesh. He seemed to shrivel into his clothes, a collapsed bundle in his chair, and his greasy face started perspiring from every pore. His last defence was down. The accusing gleam of the silver watch, and the further terror of Kurt Quillan and the quivering threat of that leashed force that moved with Kurt wherever he went, was too great an offensive for Louie to endure without abject surrender.

"I—I can't tell you nothin', because I don't know no more than you do. But I—" He gulped, and swallowed, and took a new start: "I'll throw you what I found. That—that watch wath in an old tomato can in my woodthhed. I gueth I'd never found it, but Bill told me to take a good look around, tho I looked into everything."

"Let's see it," Stagg interposed, and held out his hand. "Side bothering you much, Kurt?"

"Sore as the devil, Bill. Louie, you haven't invited me, but I'm going to eat some of this gravy and whatever I can manage with this jaw. I need nourishment. Where do we go to see what you have to show us?"

"Up—up back of the barn, in a canyon. Thure —you—you help yourthelf, Kurt. I'll wait. I—I don't want nothin' to eat, now."

Stagg inspected the watch and dropped it into his pocket. "You found it in a can in your wood-shed, eh? About when was this, Louie?"

"Yethderday mornin', after I got the chicken cooked and thtarted lookin'. I put it right back in the can, and I thought of buryin' it right then, but I wath too crathy to thee if there wath any-thing elthe like that around. And I went on lookin', but I—I didn't find nothin' elthe till I come to—to the canyon."

"Well, he won't get anywhere trying to frame you, Louie, whoever he is." With a quiet diplo-macy to be expected from his quick intelligence, Stagg turned the conversation into common-place channels till Kurt had appeased his hunger with the most substantial meal he had yet eaten since the day his jaw was broken, and Kurt rose at last, turning his faint smile on Louie.

"All right, Louie. Thanks a lot. Either I've forgotten what good grub tastes like or you're the best cook in seven States. Lead the way, Louie, and keep your shirt on."

Louie, still shrunk in his clothes, like a man in a dumb daze of fear, got up and walked out as he might if he were going to his own hanging.

He went into the barn for the shovel. They got their mounts, and Louie led the way up the sloping terrain beyond the barn for about a mile, till they were deep in a narrow canyon, and the going became a little difficult for the horses they rode. Then they came abruptly to the end of the canyon, which was a long slide of loose shale and coarse-grained earth. As they drew their horses to a halt, Louie gestured for them to dismount, and pointed with a shaking hand toward a spot nearly in the centre of the base of the slide.

"D-dig there. You won't need to—to dig very far."

Both Quillan and Stagg were inwardly certain of what they would find, they were really seeking mere confirmation of their own convictions. Therefore neither one of them was greatly surprised when Stagg, wielding the shovel and insisting that Kurt consider his injured side, uncovered the body of Owen Barnes. There was little shock in the simple fact of Barnes's death. It was the condition of the body that made Stagg feel a sick wave at the pit of his stomach, and caused Kurt to turn his gaze away.

Barnes's lips were drawn back from the row of upper teeth crowned with gold. The entire face was seared and mutilated by knife slashes and deep burns. Both hands and feet were still tied tightly together. And Stagg remembered how Louie had said, "you'd kill a man quick and clean, anyhow—you wouldn't torture him."

"Cottrelle ith buried jutht beyond him," Louie volunteered shakily, "if you want to dig any more. I looked. There'th not much left of Cottrelle."

"We'll take your word for it," Stagg replied, and began to shovel the earth back over Barnes's mutilated body. "How did you happen to find this, Louie? And when did you find it?"

"About two hourth after I found that watch. I —well—Oh, don't make me tell it! Don't make me thay any more!"

Louie shrank against the rough bole of a tree behind him, and again he was on the verge of gibbering horror. Kurt Quillan stepped up to him; he laid a hand on either of Louie's thin shoulders, and his diamond-hard blue eyes commanded Louie's gaze, forcing Louie's one good eye to raise, in spite of its reluctance, to meet his. For a long-drawn minute Kurt held the little man's gaze, and Louie straightened a bit, and some of the terror subsided in his greasy dark face; it blanked, and nearly all expression went out of it.

Louie le Grande was half hypnotized by that steady, unwinking stare with all of Kurt's vibrating magnetic force behind it, but he didn't realize it. Then Kurt spoke, softly, as one speaks in a room where people are asleep and must not be disturbed.

"Louie, no one is going to know about this till I have gotten you safely hidden where no man can find you, and you will stay hidden there till we get the man behind all this, and you're cleared of every shadow of suspicion. You can depend on that. But we have to know everything you can tell us, before I take you there. Now don't be silly. Go on and tell what you've been hiding, and let's get to work on this business before the fellow tries to give us the slip. Don't leave anything out this time."

Louie stood motionless, held by that still gaze, but he answered without the least hesitation: "I wath jutht lookin' along back of the barn, and I heard thomethin' that thounded like a dog, thort of groanin' and thlobberin', like thomebody wath half killin' it. I didn't know how any dog could be up here, and I thtarted to follow the thound. It kept gettin' weaker ath I come nearer, and I thought maybe a cougar had got thomethin' down. I thneaked along and kept under cover tho I wouldn't attract hith attention, and I got clear to the edge of the canyon before I thaw what it wath.

"And it wath a man, that man that wearth chapth like mine, and he had that red bandanna over hith fathe, and he looked tho much like me that it wath almotht like watchin' mythelf, and what he had down there wathn't any dog. It wath another man—it wath Barnth, tied up jutht like you thaw him. And the other fella had a little fire, and he had a runnin' iron, red-hot, and he wath thwipin' it acroth Barnth' fathe. I wath goin' to thock a big rock at him, and try to hit him, and then he picked up a big rock himthelf, and whacked Barnth on the thide of the head. Barnth jutht quit groanin' and laid thtill.

"Then I got thick, and for a few minuteth I couldn't move, and when I thort of come to mythelf the fella in the red chapth wath diggin' that hole to bury Barnth. I got away from there, and I'd have given anything I've got if Bill had been here. There wathn't a thoul I could get to help round that fella up. Lon and hith boyth had gone away early in the mornin' with a herd, I thaw 'em go, but I went over there anyway, hopin' thome of 'em would be back. But they wathn't. Nobody come home over there till late in the afternoon, when Jothay Thancheth thowed up. And it wath too late then. I thneaked up the canyon two timeth after that, and there wathn't no thign of anything. The fella'd buried Barnth, and even all trathe of hith fire wath gone."

"Did you tell Sanchez about it?" Kurt asked.

"No. I—I wath afraid to. It had come to me by then how it wath going to look to everybody elthe. I hadn't a thoul to back me up, to thwear that I wath thome where elthe when that killin' wath goin' on. Not a man home on the L I; Lon and half the boyth wath away over to the Theven Up, the retht of the L I boyth gone to Theco Thpringth; Bill wath gone. I wath here all by mythelf."

"You would be," Kurt's chill tones were dry, and he dropped his hands from Louie's shoulders, and the right hand lingered for an instant in a reassuring grip. "Don't you suppose that the devil who is clever enough to have planned and executed this whole thing is also smart enough to have laid a frame like this on you, Louie, when you couldn't dig up the shadow of an alibi, or bring forth a witness to testify to your innocence? It's all clear as mud, Louie. He had means of knowing that Bill had gone, that all the hands of the L I would be absent for the day, away out of the territory where they couldn't possibly get back in time to catch him.

"And with the reputation you've got in this country, Louie—it's almost as good as mine—if you would make the statement that you saw a man dressed like you, doing what was done to

Barnes, on your own ranch, burying Barnes in your own canyon, how many people would believe you? Not a soul, Louie. Not one. Only Bill and me. And the only proof we have to support your assertions is that the fellow was seen in that get-up, posing as you, when you were with Jerry Hulan rounding up strays. And who saw him at that time? Only me. The only word you'd have that the man had been seen when he couldn't be you, is mine. And it's no damned good in the Seco!

"The only man who would accept my word and say he believed me, is Bill. And do you think that would help any? Not now, Louie; not after Bill took me in the way he did, with the inference clear that he was trying to save my worthless hide. Nobody would believe anything Bill said to back me up, when he had only my word for something I'd seen, and I was trying to back up some wild things you'd told to save yourself. It's a perfect set-up, Louie. It's a fool-proof trap. And it's got us both—unless we can catch the man running around in red chaps. If he should get away, and all this should come to light, even Lon wouldn't believe any more that the fellow he saw branding his stuff wasn't you.

"Didn't you yourself say that the fellow looked so much like you that it was like seeing yourself? We've got only one hope, Louie. To catch him before it's too late. And we're going to make one mighty effort to do it.

"Bill." Kurt swung his gaze to Stagg, who stood leaning on the shovel, his huge body humped in a slouching pose, listening intently. "I'm going to take Louie and hit for the cave in Lobo Pass. I'm going to hide Louie there till this is all over. You start out gathering up a posse that will sweep this range from one end to the other. Start with Lon. Tell him just what's what, and tell him to have his boys ready to ride the minute they show up this afternoon.

"Then you high-tail it for the Circle G. Tell Pete, and have him send men to the Cross Bar, the L-Over-S, and the Seven Up. Have the whole lot of 'em start the sweep at daylight in the morning. They'll have all night to get in position. Have the boys from the L-Over-S and the Cross Bar string across the open range to the south, from Arroyo to Seco Springs. Have the Circle G and Seven Up men string along the east end of the range from the Circle G down. Have the L I men string across the west end, from the L I down.

"At daylight, tell 'em to start closing in, and sweep that range as clean as a hound's tooth. If that sweet-scented trouble maker is on this range, they'll have him by to-morrow night.

"Louie and I will hit straight across the open range and cut Seco Trail above the north-west edge of the Circle G, and be at Lobo Pass before dark. The minute I've got Louie safe, I'll turn back. By daylight I'll be posted at the north of the open range in the hills. Believe me, Bill, I know those hills. I know just about how far anybody can get back in them, and where the mountains will stop anything that can't climb like a cougar or soar like a buzzard. That fellow's still here, because he hasn't finished what he started. With a cordon like that, we have to get him."

"Holy cow!" breathed Louie. "You should have been a general."

"There are a good many things I should have been, Louie." Kurt's voice was singing-hard with bitterness. "I may be a corpse by to-morrow night—but if I leave a clean slate, I'll ask nothing more."

"You're walking right into it," said Stagg heavily. "You're going to tear everything wide open, if you work it that way. And you probably will dig up things you never dreamed were there. This man in the red chaps is mixed up in your life somewhere, Kurt. It's clear that he stole both that wedding certificate and the deed to the L-Over-S years ago, and planted them there in Lon's house, never dreaming Louie would walk off with them. Think what you're doing before you start a wholesale blow-up like that, because very probably you haven't a chance to come out of it alive."

"I'll have to play it the way I see it, Bill." Kurt's eyes were quite cold, that chill clean blue which no man could read. "If I ever clean the slate, it's got to be before the whole damned range. There's no other way. She said—she said it would still be worth it, Bill; and if it took me out of this world, there is another world, and she'd meet me there some day. Will you do what I asked you to do?"

"Yes." Stagg straightened, and started along the canyon bed toward the horses. "You and Louie get started for Lobo Pass. I'll go over to see Lon as soon as we get back to the cabin."

Less than an hour later, Louie and Kurt Quillan left the Crazy L, headed straight across the northern edge of the open range for the Seco Trail. Louie's legs were encased by the ragged old red chaps. His thin shoulders drooped a little under his faded and patched old blue shirt. His greasy face was shaded by the low-crowned old stained tan hat crowded down onto his black hair.

Kurt rode straight and at ease in the saddle, and his garb differed from its usual habit only in that he wore Stagg's gun belts, and a grey shirt the doctor had lent him to replace the blue shirt Ivey's bullet and his own blood had ruined. Bill Stagg was riding across the open field to Lon Ivey's stone house half hidden in the towering oaks.

CHAPTER XIII
THE VALLEY OF DEATH

IVEY opened the door to Bill's knock with a pleased smile on his lean, sunburned face, and the eyes that looked so like fine-grained moss agate lighted with pleasure. "Come right in, Bill. I'm glad to see you again. You look in a serious mood. Anything wrong now?"

Stagg barely stepped inside the door and explained rapidly about the finding of Barnes's body, and what Louie had seen and heard.

Ivey paled and shook his head. "By gonnies, Bill, that's awful! Seems like we ought to do something right away!"

"We're going to. Oh, hello, José." His gaze swerved to greet Sanchez, who appeared from behind a tall cupboard across the room, his mouth slack behind his enormous jaw. Stagg went on to outline the plan for throwing a cordon around the entire range. "And if the devil can get away from that, we might as well quit. Will all your men be home in time, Lon? Or had I better go by Seco Springs and tell them?"

"No need of your going that far out of your way, Bill. They'll be home before dark, and we'll start runnin' our string right down the west end of the range here. We'll be ready to move at daylight, and by gonnies, you can depend on us. I'm plumb glad you've got Louie and Kurt safe out of the way. We can't make no mistake getting the wrong man in red chaps now. I swan, that's a smart scheme, Bill."

"Kurt planned it. Well, I'll get going for the Circle G, Lon. Be seeing you somewhere tomorrow."

And he did not realize till some time afterward that he had neglected to say that Kurt himself would be back at dawn to take his post to the north of the open range in the hills. Not that he could see how it mattered. By the time the men reached the place where Kurt would be, something would have come to light, somehow. Kurt might even have a better chance to fight his way through if no one knew he was there.

Down in Arroyo, Doctor Mordan laid aside a prescription he was filling to answer an urgent knock at the door. On the porch he found one of the ranch hands of the Seven Up.

"Mornin', doc," the Seven Up man greeted him hurriedly. "Can you come right over to the ranch? Hank's leg is nearly drivin' him crazy. Swellin' and discolourin' and the missus says she's afraid it's gettin' infected again."

"Well, boy!" The doctor's thin, wind-seamed face wrinkled in a scowl. "If that man isn't having a mean time with his leg. I'll get my kit and hitch up and come right along."

"Thanks. I'll tell him you're on the way."

The Seven Up man went down the steps, and the doctor closed the door and turned back into his office room to face Micky.

"What's the matter with the man's leg, Uncle Dan?"

"Broke it. Bronc threw him. This is the third time it's got infected. I came nearly having to amputate it, and if this keeps up I may have to do it yet to save Hank's life. You'd better go along with me, Micky. We can be back by midnight."

"Yes, I'll go, of course. Only—I was thinking about Kurt. If he should come here, needing you again—hurt. There's no telling what may happen to him, how soon he might be—"

"Now, listen to me, my dear." The doctor laid one arm around her shoulders, and with the other hand raised her face to meet his gaze. "There is such a thing as destiny. If that boy is to die, so he can face his Maker with the blood wiped from his hands, neither you nor I can change it. If there is hope for him to win out of such a hopeless situation, his Maker will see to that also. I've heard that most doctors become rank materialists, but I still believe in my God, and though His way may not always seem my way, I know that He has never let me down, and that somehow whatever He wills is best. You'll have to trust Him; a higher hand than ours is needed to set this thing straight.

"Kurt's been gone since last night, and evidently nothing has happened to him yet. He's taken care of himself long enough to keep on doing it. I don't believe anything is going to work out of this affair so quickly; it's going to take several days. You go over to Jay Stokes, and tell him we have to go to save Hank Braun's life if possible. Tell him to keep an eye on the house here, and if anybody shows up to come over and investigate. Tell him to do his best with first aid if anybody injured comes looking for me. I'll have the team hitched by the time you get back."

Eight hours later, in the waning afternoon, Kurt Quillan and Louie le Grande were nearing Lobo Pass. They rode straight into a blast of gunfire levelled on them from ambush. Louie choked out a cry, lurched to one side, and barely had presence of mind and time enough to jerk his feet free of the stirrups as he fell from the saddle and hurtled to the ground, shot through the chest. Kurt felt the impact of two bullets, one in the flesh of his thigh, and one in his upper arm. He pulled his feet free and threw himself to the ground.

Then both guns were out, raking the thick brush from which the attack had come. Beyond the brush the crashing of branches sounded faintly through Quillan's gunfire, then the drum of the hoofs of a hard-ridden horse. Quillan holstered his guns.

"So, this is where he's got to! Louie! Are you badly hurt?"

"Through the chetht," Louie gulped, breathing heavily. "I gueth I'm done for."

"Not if I can help it. We aren't more than a couple of miles above the Seven Up buildings. I can see the roof of the ranch house from here. Maybe Mrs. Ryan can do something for you, and if the men aren't all gone to join the posse already we can send one for the doctor. Easy, now, Louie; I'll be as careful as I can."

He lifted the little man in his arms, walked across to the Arabian, and managed to get into the saddle, and turned the brown horse towards the Seven Up to the south, cradling Louie in his arms. Within forty minutes he was at the ranch-house door, knocking for admittance, and Mrs. Ryan came to open the door, and started back at what she saw.

"My heavens, boys! Whatever has happened? Come in, quick; you can barely stand up, you poor boy!"

Kurt advanced into the room, weaving a little, not quite steady on his feet. "I'm Kurt Quillan, Mrs. Ryan. This is Louie le Grande. He's shot through the chest, pretty badly, I'm afraid. Can you possibly do anything for him, and send one of your men for the doctor?"

"The doctor's here," answered Mrs. Ryan quickly. "He came to fix Hank's leg; been here

216

nearly an hour. Bring Louie this way; take him into that room and lay him on the bed. I'll call the doctor." She went swiftly into the rooms beyond, without a backward look, to where the doctor and Micky were finishing a glass of milk and some apple pie she had set out for them on the little round table in the living room.

Mordan looked up in inquiry at her suddenly excited air. "Something wrong, Mrs. Ryan? Violence seems to follow me sometimes."

"Lispy Louie," said Mrs. Ryan breathlessly. "That queer little man from the Crazy L; he's out there, doctor. Shot through the chest. He looks terrible bad. And who do you think brought him? The outlaw, Kurt Quillan! He's kind of shaky, too; looks as if he may be shot, but I couldn't see where."

The doctor got quickly to his feet, and his gaze sought his niece's face, and though neither spoke, there passed between them one freighted word—destiny. Then the doctor was gone, toward the room where Mrs. Ryan pointed, Micky close at his side, and Mrs. Ryan stared in a kind of bewildered blankness at such sudden motion, and followed.

Kurt was sitting on the edge of the bed beside Louie when the doctor came into the room, and his gaze leaped beyond Mordan's long thin figure to Micky; he had not expected to see her there.

The room was filled with a tense silence.

Mordan's trained eyes swept over Kurt, saw the hole in his shirt sleeve and the small stain of blood there, caught sight of the hole in his leather chaps and the dark rim of blood that had seeped through it, and saw no other signs of injury, and passed on to Louie, as he approached and bent over the bed.

"Tell the truth, doc." Louie was breathing heavily. "Am I going to die?"

The doctor made a swift, cursory examination before he answered, then he straightened, and reached for the kit he had brought from the kitchen. "Honestly, Louie. I don't know. You may die, you may live. The chances are about even. I'll know better after I locate the bullet. It's still in you. Kurt, can you still walk?"

"Gosh, yes! I've only a couple of scratches."

"I'll be the judge of that. Go out into the other room; get your chaps off and lie down on the couch. Stay there till I come out. Micky, cut his pants away from the thigh, and take a look at his arm. You'd better go on out too, Mrs. Ryan. I prefer to take care of Louie alone. I'll be with you as quickly as I can. No arguments, Kurt. Get along, all of you."

He stood erect by the bed, his mouth pursed dubiously under his white moustache, until they had left the room, then he again bent over Louie le Grande.

"Louie," he said quietly, "you'll have to take

218

this as well as you can. I brought some ether with me, but I had to use it on Hank, and I'd be afraid to use it on you anyway. If you can hang on till we get that bullet out, we'll know where we are."

"I can—hang on." Louie's cocked eye looked a little glazed, but his good eye held steady on the doctor's face. "But if I've got—to die, I want to know it—in time. I want to talk—to thomebody."

"What about?" said Mordan sharply.

"About the man—in the red chapth. I know who he ith. I been thinkin'—and I know. Nobody'd believe me. But I know. And I know thomething about Kurt—that I've got to tell. I don't want to thay nothin' unleth I have to. But if I've got to die—I want to know it."

"I give you my word that you shall know, Louie. Now don't talk any more. Lie still. I won't hurt you any more than I have to."

Louie closed his eyes and set himself to endure, and when it was done, and Mordan went out into the other room, the doctor's thin face looked weary, and there was perspiration on his forehead and in the white moustache.

In that other room, as the three had quitted Louie's room at the doctor's order, Micky had waited with tense breath, as Quillan removed his gun belts and chaps, and Mrs. Ryan had stood about in helpless anxiety, and still none of them had found any words.

Then Kurt walked unsteadily to the couch and

dropped onto it, and spoke to Mrs. Ryan, his eyes avoiding Micky.

"Have your men gone to join the posse yet, Mrs. Ryan?"

"Why, no, they haven't. We only got the word a few minutes ago. They'll be ready pretty soon."

"Tell them not to go. The man we want is north of this ranch. He was the one who fired on Louie and me. Tell Pat and the boys to cut him off from the pass, and send one of the boys to tell the posse to swing this way and trap him from the west.

"Oh! Oh, dear! I—yes, I'll go right out and tell Pat. Is there any danger of that man coming here?"

"I hardly think so. Will you tell the boys to get going as quick as they can?"

She nodded and scurried out of the room, and Kurt's gaze lifted to meet Micky's amber eyes. "Micky! I didn't want to speak to you first with any one else around. I did get to see you again, didn't I?"

"Kurt!" She leaned over him and began rolling up his sleeve to look at the wound on his arm. "Why are you over here? What's happened?"

These three things happened simultaneously: while Micky bent above Kurt, listening to his report of what had taken place since he had last left Arroyo, while Doctor Mordan worked to extract the bullet from Louie le Grande's chest,

Lon Ivey's men started on their way to draw their part of the cordon at the west edge of the range. They filed past the house and the last man in the line pulled his mount to a halt by the rear porch, where the saddled horses belonging to Sanchez and Ivey were standing.

"Hey, boss! We're all ready!"

Sanchez's heavy-jawed face peered out the window, turned away, and Sanchez's heavy voice called into the part of the house beyond the kitchen. "The boys is all ready to ride, boss. You going now?"

Ivey's voice came back impatiently: "Waal, I swan, José, do you have to hurry me all the time? Of course I'm coming now. I don't hanker to be left out of this round-up."

José thrust his enormous jaw out the door. "Yeah. He says we'll be right along."

"Uh-huh. I heard him. We won't wait. You two are going to take the top of the string opposite the Crazy L anyhow. Be seeing you, José."

At almost the same time, a very little later, Pete Gulick was saying to Bill Stagg. "Well, we got our guns all oiled up good, by Jiminy! We get him now, Bill. Jerry must be down by de L-Over-S already."

Jerry was. He had, in passing, left word at the Cross Bar. And he had just finished repeating instructions to Rocky Andover. And Rocky was saying with a dubious frown:

"By glory, Jerry, there's something screwy about this whole business. But I'm willing to take our men and do our part, if we can run that fellow down. I wish Coke was here, damn it. I got to worrying after Kurt was here last night, and I just slipped into Arroyo and sent Coke a wire from the railroad station. But he may not have got it. I wish he'd show up. I feel as if I was sitting on a keg of giant powder."

And all of this was taking place at about the time Doctor Mordan walked out of Louie's room with perspiration on his forehead and upper lip.

"He's a game little devil," the doctor said as he joined Micky beside the couch where Kurt lay. "I believe he's got more than an even chance at that. And now what have I got to do to keep you from losing some more blood you can't spare?" He leaned to look at the place on Kurt's thigh, where Micky had cut away a section of the dark-blue cloth, exposing the flesh. The wound extended through the flesh from the back to the fore, on the outside of the thigh, about six inches above the knee. "Never even bored a muscle," Mordan grunted. "You certainly are lucky. Mrs. Ryan can get you—oh, here you are, Mrs. Ryan."

"Yes, doctor. I went out to tell Pat and the boys—and they said they'd cut off the pass right away—and one of the boys is already off to the Circle G—and—what did you want, doctor?"

Mordan's thin face relaxed into a humorous

smile. "Calm down, Mrs. Ryan. I'll have to be giving you a bromide the next thing you know. I wanted you to get an extra pair of Pat's overalls for Kurt. Micky's ruined his pants. Don't bank on seeing the overalls again. Look what he did to the sleeve of that shirt I let him have. It doesn't pay to lend your clothes to that boy."

The dressing of the wounds was neither a complicated nor lengthy task. The score on the arm had barely burned through the layers of skin. When the dressings were done, Kurt sat up on the couch, swinging his legs to the floor. Mrs. Ryan brought a pair of Pat Ryan's overalls, and Kurt stepped into an adjoining room to put them on. He came out with his leather chaps over the overalls, and the gun belts again slung about his waist.

While Kurt was dressing, the doctor and Micky had gone in to see Louie. Louie's good eye stared up anxiously:

"Am I goin' to die, doc?"

Mordan picked up the little man's wrist and counted his pulse. "Your pulse is much stronger, Louie. I can't be sure yet, but I don't believe you're going to die. Your chances are getting better every minute. Anything you want?"

"Could I talk to Mithuth Ryan for a minute?"

"You'd better not do any talking yet for a while, Louie. You take it perfectly easy, and I'll tell you when you can talk."

Then Kurt came in the door and looked down

at Louie. "Is he—does he stand a pretty good chance, doctor?"

"Yes, he does. He's going to come out of it, I believe. And we're all going to clear out of here and let him keep quiet."

By that time the dusk was falling, and as the three of them went quietly out of the bedroom and paused to see Mrs. Ryan lighting a lamp in the living room, Kurt's voice swept coolly through the silence.

"I'm going to cut up through to the north where that fellow jumped Louie and me. The men from the other side of the range can't get here much before morning. I might have a long chance of running into him again, but I'll be looking for him this time. I wonder if I could get a fresh horse from you, Mrs. Ryan? Mine has been going it rather steadily for the last two days."

Mrs. Ryan told him that all of the men were gone now, even Pat, but there were two good horses still in the barn, and he could take his choice. He stared blindly into Micky's delicate face, as if he would imprint forever upon his memory some vision he never expected to view again, and passed from the room with that smooth-flowing noiseless stride, and behind him there seemed a sudden emptiness, as if some pulsing force had abruptly vanished from the air, leaving the atmosphere dull and leaden.

Mrs. Ryan's gaze passed over the pale-blond

waves of Micky's hair, to the light of unendurable pain in the amber eyes, and the woman's worried stumbling tongue whispered six appalled words:

"Oh, my dear, you love him!"

As the doctor sank into a chair and hid his grey eyes behind a thin veined hand, Micky choked back a sob, whirled, and ran out of the room and out of the house.

When Kurt came from the barn with a Seven Up horse, leaving the weary Arabian in a quiet stall, the girl was waiting for him in the deepening dusk, and he saw her at first as something that he dreamed was there, till she moved and spoke, and addressed him quietly:

"Kurt, I want to walk with you a little way. That's all."

For the first time he reached out and touched her intentionally, at the behest of emotion. He placed one arm around her, and they walked down the lane, past the house together, in silence, until they came to the edge of the forest strip beside which he intended to turn to the north. He slowed his steps there and turned to face her, and he could see her pale forehead and hair clearly in the dusk.

He laid his cheek against hers, and she felt the quivering force that lived in him, closing around her like something tangible, yet he made no other move.

"Maybe." His voice was a muted whisper. "Just—maybe. Three from eight leaves five."

Then he released her, and seemed to move like a shadow from her, and onto the horse's back, and was gone up the dim north branch road that led along the edge of the forest strip. She had no need to ask what he meant. Neither of them wanted it put into words. Three from eight. One in the arm, and one in the side, and one in the thigh. She stood watching till he vanished into the night, and turned to go back to the house and was shocked and shaken to wild stillness by a burst of sound.

The crash of a revolver shot, followed by another. The pound of the feet of a frightened horse, running.

She thought she must have stood there an eternity before her terror-stiffened muscles would give. In reality it was scarcely three ticks of a watch before she whirled and ran madly along the tree belt, to come to a swaying stop at sight of a dark figure sprawled face downward in the dust at the edge of the road.

She flung herself down beside him, and reached a hand to his face, and felt his blood upon her fingers.

"Kurt—Kurt—"

The words choked off as two lean hard arms snatched her up from behind and a man's calloused hand clamped over her mouth. She felt herself dragged back as the man doubled her up in his arms and started along the road with her. She struggled to free herself and the man halted and deliberately struck her on the side of the head with a doubled fist, knocking her senseless.

Inside the house, Mrs. Ryan was stoking the stove against the evening chill with a little wood the doctor had brought in. She shut the stove door with a bang, and Mordan turned his head quickly, frowning. "Did that door make all that noise?"

"No." Mrs. Ryan's eyes dilated, startled. "That came from outside, somewhere. It sounded like a shot."

From the bedroom Louie called: "Doc. Doc! Thomebodyth thhootin' outthide. Can I talk to Mithuth Ryan now."

"No, you can't talk to anybody yet! I don't believe that was a shot, was it? Maybe it was. But the slam of that stove door disguised it to my hearing. Micky will know, she'll hear it clearly enough. She can tell us when she comes in. But I don't see how it would be a shot unless Kurt was shooting at something." He got up and went to the door of the bedroom. "Louie, what's so important about your talking to Mrs. Ryan? Can't it wait till you're a little better?"

"I thuppothe tho, but I jutht wanted to athk her a question."

"Let him ask it, doctor, and then he'll stop worrying," said Mrs. Ryan, at Mordan's elbow. "What is it, Louie?"

227

"Wath Lon Ivey with the boyth when they brought the herd yethterday?"

"Why, yes, he was, Louie. Why?"

Louie sighed. "I gueth thatth no good then. You thee, I got to thinkin' it wath Lon Ivey doin' all thith dirty work. I wath thure of it. But if he wath here when that fella wath killin' Barnth, I'm all off again."

"You go to sleep, Louie," said Mordan dryly. "You'll be getting delirious next. Come and sit down, Mrs. Ryan. I wish Micky would hurry in. I'd like to know if she heard anything."

The doctor and Mrs. Ryan had barely returned to their seats, when the front door swung open, and Kurt lurched in, his chestnut hair gleaming in the lamplight, his hat gone, dust on his face and blood running down the side of his head.

"Did Micky come back?" he asked tersely.

Mrs. Ryan rose, gaping, and Mordan's lean body leaped erect.

That was answer enough. Kurt's cold eyes knew a flame that had never lighted them before. "Don't get panicky! He's as smooth an article as ever lived. He crept right down to the house, knowing the men were all up to the north looking for him. Dusk, and his aim was bad, I suppose. He only succeeded in taking a little nick out of my scalp. I threw myself off my horse and hit a rock, and the rock knocked me out. When I came to my horse had run off and Micky didn't answer anywhere, and I thought—I'll saddle up the other horse in the barn. If I can't bring her back, I won't come myself."

The doctor sank limply into his chair as Kurt flashed out the door and Mrs. Ryan began to tremble.

"Oh, doctor, that poor child—and that awful man—"

"Keep still!" said Mordan harshly. "We can't let ourselves go to pieces!"

Mrs. Ryan sat down, and gripped her shaking hands together, then started to attention. "What? What did you say, doctor?"

But Mordan's eyes were closed, and his lips were moving steadily as if in prayer to some power beyond which he had no recourse.

Across miles and space, a Seven Up man rode hard into the yard of the Circle G and spoke a tense message to the men gathered there. "Don't wait till morning and work to the west. Start now. Close in to the east. He's in the hills somewhere above the Seven Up. We're cutting off his way to the pass. Send word to the Cross Bar and the L-Over-S and the L I."

And Pete Gulick cursed, and his round fat face reddened with excitement. "Gus, you take der L-Over-S. Benny, you go mit der L I. Gus could stop also by der Cross Bar. See how fast you could ride, yet. Where was you going, Bill?"

"To the Seven Up, Pete. There's something I forgot to ask Kurt."

"Well, by Jiminy!" said the fat little Dutchman. And he turned to watch Stagg, who loomed like a big dark blot against the white patch in the night that was Skater, as Stagg heaved himself into the saddle and turned the white gelding toward the east.

Two other men rode from the Circle G, one to the south, and one to the west. And into the hills above the Seven Up and to the west of the Seven Up, another man rode, leading a horse on which a girl was bound into the saddle.

The girl returned to consciousness to find her hands tied behind her, a handkerchief over her mouth, and she strained her eyes to distinguish the figure of the man on the horse ahead of her. She could make little of him in the dim moonlight, save the outline of a small body, a flat-crowned hat, and the ragged edges of angora chaps. Her brain cleared slowly, her head ached, and she felt a sick certainty that Kurt had been dead as he lay there in the road.

She had no idea how long a time has passed since the man on the horse ahead had torn her away from Kurt's senseless body. She thought the present time must be at least early morning. The moon was low and there was but a faint light from the stars, when the man ahead finally brought both horses to a stop in a thick grove of pines within which there was a small clearing. He dismounted, walked back to her horse, and spoke curtly.

"Don't make any trouble and you won't get hurt."

He untied the ropes that bound her feet, lifted her to the ground, gripped her arm, and guided her to a tree. There was a log in front of the tree. Either he knew his way about, or he could see like a cat in the dark.

"Sit down," he commanded. "On that log." He felt about for the log with his foot, and pushed her against it. She relaxed helplessly upon it, sitting rigidly upright, and her lips set angrily behind the constricting handkerchief as she felt him tying her ankles to the log, by a stub that grew from it. She could feel the stub prodding her ankle bone. He stepped back, and she could not even distinguish the bulk of his figure in the darkness. The growth of the trees shut out even the dim light of the stars.

"What possible excuse could you have for taking me?" Micky demanded.

The man answered with a mirthless laugh: "To scare the devil out of that fool who's so hard to kill, and make him follow so I can get a chance at him. Shut up."

She heard the sound of his feet moving about, the crack of breaking limbs, the rasp of a match. Her voice sharpened. "Are you building a fire?

Why?" Something in the thought was unexplainably sinister.

He laughed again. "I didn't get Quillan with that last shot. I didn't mean to. I just wanted to get him out of the way till I got my hands on you. He'll be right on our trail. I'm just making a little guide light. You'll be right in it. You won't be able to yell and warn him. I'll be on the ground, near the fire, gun ready, but I'll look sound asleep. The minute he steps into sight, to hold me up and let you loose, I'll have him. And what I did to Barnes won't be a patch on what I'll do to Quillan."

Micky felt numbness creeping over her. The idea was of a complexion with all he had done. Killing Kurt wasn't enough. He wanted to capture him and torture him. Yet her own clear-thinking brain fought to keep clear of panic. Kurt's head had been wet with blood, yet the man who had shot him had been close enough to see him fall in the gathering dusk. He was certain Kurt had not been severely injured. He was quite as certain Kurt would follow him. So far he was arguing logically enough. But no intelligence can grant another intelligence further shrewdness than that of which it itself is capable, and his brain power belonged to a far lower level than that of Kurt Quillan. Somewhere along that trail between, Kurt might out-think him.

She sat motionless, waiting tensely till the fire

should cast its glow over the little clearing, but when the flames leaped up at last, their revelation availed her little. His face was completely covered by a red bandanna handkerchief. His hat was pulled low over his eyes. She could see in the glow as the flames grew brighter that the hat was low-crowned, tan, stained and old, his shirt was a faded-blue, his ragged chaps as red as the hide of a sorrel horse.

She wondered if it were possible that he could be negligent or thoughtless enough to leave her as she was, without adding some sort of gag to that utterly ineffectual handkerchief tied about her mouth. Or would it be possible for her to keep his attention engaged long enough to make enough startling remarks and ask enough appalling questions to keep him from thinking of it, or to keep him from thinking of anything else much, till Kurt had time to draw close enough and hear their voices, and be warned? She looked back over her pathological experience, and she weighed one reaction against another.

Men were inclined to think that women were always asking fool questions and making heedless remarks; they weren't entirely wrong in that, either. But sometimes the fool question and heedless remarks served a cunning wit. More than one had shrewdly employed that ruse, and played the dumb Dora or the nosey Nora to her own appreciative gain. But Micky told herself that she would top that by playing foolhardy Flora, and she might win by a nose, having nothing to lose. She said abruptly:

"Why did you torture Barnes? Why didn't you simply kill him and be done with it?"

The man jerked upright, whirled and stood still, and she knew he was peering sharply at her through the thin folds of the bandanna. He said harshly:

"To pay him off for something he did to me once. For a letter he wrote that made me a lot of hell. You're asking dangerous questions."

"What's dangerous about it?" Micky returned deliberately. "What does it matter how much more I know? I already know who you are. I recognized your voice. I can't see why somebody hasn't guessed your identity before." Which were the remarks of nosey Nora.

He still stood utterly still. She knew her life wasn't worth a great deal right about then, but she sat frozenly erect, staring toward his hidden face. Then he relaxed, and once more he laughed.

"You couldn't recognize my voice. You never heard it before. And even if you'd heard it, I'm not talking like I always do. I'm being very careful about that. You never saw me in your life. Who do you think I am?"

"You're Frank Cross, or Lon Ivey, or Coke Laughlin. Kurt says you have to be one of the three." That was dumb Dora. "Kurt told me all he'd found out in the last few days, down at the Seven Up this evening. So I know. And Lon Ivey is with the posse clear across the range, and Coke Laughlin went to Madder Junction, so you must be Frank Cross." Dumb Dora was doing very well.

He still did not move. He still did not evidence by any sign what reaction he might have felt toward her words. Then he shrugged suddenly, and sneered his contempt. "You've got me. But it won't do any good. I was going to let you loose, after I'd made short work of Kurt Quillan. But you can both be dumped into the same hole now."

Foolhardy Flora came to the rescue in that demoralizing moment. Micky answered him with equal contempt. "And that will put you in a hole, Mr. Cross. It is conceivable that if you should kill Kurt Quillan, who has already been condemned as an outlaw, and if the man in red chaps should then disappear from the face of the range, the men of the Seco might be inclined to get over their rage and forget it. But if you kill me as you once killed Bess Quillan, you won't be able to go far enough or fast enough to get away from them. You probably haven't brains enough to see that."

"I'm a couple of jumps ahead of you. I didn't kill Bess Quillan. Lem Strickland did. Ask Lon Ivey. You're pretty smart. Killing you off might get me in a bad hole, at that. And if I let you live—hm-m-m. I'm clear. I can bring up alibis by the dozen."

"I get you, Mr. Cross," said Micky, and her voice burned with a loathing and scorn that was not at all assumed. "You mean you can prove by some of your ranch hands that you have been some place else whenever these atrocities have occurred. You've probably been using your ignorant and innocent cowboys as dupes and cat's-paws; you could easily make them believe you were right there on your ranch, when you were in reality many miles away. And that's what you did do, isn't it?"

Again the short harsh laugh. "You are smart, and no fooling about it. That's what I did, all right. I kind of admire you, at that. I like people that's smart."

"So do I," returned Micky, with exactly the right amount of grudging approval and flaying contempt. "I've always admired people who were capable of doing clever things. I think you are probably the most brutal and cruel person who ever lived, and likely the lowest, but I can't help giving you credit for the way you've carried on this one-man war of yours for seventeen years, and never slipped once. I wouldn't have believed it possible."

Which laid dumb Dora and nosey Nora in the discard, and should have made foolhardy Flora ashamed of herself. And it worked. Because there are two things to which no man is completely immune. These two things: subtly-worded flattery, and the ingratiating assurance that he has put something over on somebody who was dupe enough to swallow it whole. The man by the fire reacted as promptly and as surely as the hammer of a gun snaps into place when the thumb that has drawn it back lets it go. He said gruffly:

"I guess it wouldn't have worked if I hadn't watched myself close. I made damn near a mistake when I started hirin' men to kill Kurt off. But I couldn't risk doin' it myself then. And how did I know they'd be dumb enough to let him get 'em? Every one of 'em! It played into my hand, at that. He's got the name of killer. I can wipe him out now and the whole Seco would thank me for it."

Micky whispered under her breath. "Killing thrust upon him!"

"Eh? What?" said the man sharply.

"Nothing."

"Well, I'm goin' to gag you now. I got to be ready for him." And he drew another handkerchief from his pocket, wadding it into a gag as he approached her.

At approximately the same hour, Benny Blaine, one of the Circle G men Pete Gulick had sent

237

for the posse, having ridden hard and far for hours, came within sight of five men grouped around a small camp fire on the open range a few miles east of the Crazy L, and drew his lathered horse to a halt.

One of the men by the fire got quickly to his feet, and Benny hailed him.

"Hi, Joe. I was lookin' for you L I fellows! You're to come over to the Seven Up as fast as you can ride. Pete sent me after you. Where's the rest of 'em?"

"Lon and some of the boys has got another little fire back a piece, about a quarter mile," Joe answered. "We cleaned the Crazy L and started to work this way, and it got too dark to look any more. Moon went down. So we decided to stop and rest and eat a bite and wait for daylight. Some of the boys been takin' naps by turns, and the rest of us keepin' watch."

"Where's Frank Cross gone to?" asked Benny. "Mrs. Cross said that him and two of his boys had come over this way."

"I ain't sure," Joe answered. "I ain't seen nothin' of Frank for several hours. I guess Mort saw him last. Said he was driftin' over to the north to have a look, didn't he, Mort?"

"Yeah." Mort stared up at Benny with expressionless eyes. "I don't know what he thought he'd see up that way, but he said he had an idea about somethin'. Did Lon see him after we did?"

Joe shook his head. "He said he didn't."

"Lon's back by the next fire, you said?" asked Benny.

"Yeah," Joe answered. "When it got too dark to go on, I rode back and yelled to Lon and told him we better stop and rest a spell. He agreed with me. I asked him where Frank was, and he said he didn't know. Last he seen of him he was headed off to the north. What's happened over to the Seven Up that Pete'd send for us?"

"Just about everything that could happen," answered Benny tersely. "The fella you're lookin' for is over there somewhere. He shot Lispy Louie, and Doc Mordan said Louie's got a pretty slim chance to live. He shot Kurt, too, but he only nicked him. He's north of the ranch in the hills, and every damn man on the Seven Up, Pat included, is out lookin' for him."

"Great grief!" Joe gasped. "Why—why, it's all bustin' loose over there, and we're here yellin' down an empty barrel! You want to go back to the next fire for Lon and the boys, or shall I get 'em?"

"You go get 'em," said Benny. "I'm turnin' right here and headin' for the ranch. I got to take it kind of easy, my horse is winded some. Hightail it, Joe."

"You know it!" assured Joe, and called loudly as Benny nudged his horse into motion. "Benny! Bill Stagg showed up over your way yet?"

"He was at the Circle G when I left. Started for the Seven Up right away. Must have got there long ago."

"Yeah. So long, Benny." He wheeled to face Mort, who had risen to his feet, along with the other four L I men. "Get your gear cinched up and ready to ride while I go back and tell Lon. It won't be long now."

"Don't look like it," said Mort laconically.

Joe was already striding toward his horse. He slipped the bit into the animal's mouth, tightened the cinch, and swung into the saddle. He urged the gelding into as fast a pace as he dared, over the rough ground in the dark, and in a few moments came within sight of the dim glow of the other small fire. He called at the top of his voice:

"Hi, Lon!"

José Sanchez answered him. "He ain't here."

"Well, where in thunder is he?" Joe demanded, as he rode up to the fire. "I want him, quick!"

The other men rose and crowded up behind Sanchez. The tension in Joe's voice warned them all that some dire situation had risen.

"He got curious to see what Frank Cross was up to," answered Sanchez. "You remember when you yelled back at him that we'd better stop and rest? Well, we started a fire, and he told me to round up the rest of the boys. He didn't like the way Frank Cross was actin', said he was goin' to

240

trail him for a ways. He ain't come back yet."

"Well, go round 'em up, both of 'em," commanded Joe, and repeated Benny's message. "We got to get to the Seven Up as quick as we can make it. You boys get hold of Lon—and Frank, if you can find him, and make it fast. Me and the other boys'll get started right now. Don't waste no time talkin' about it, José."

"We won't." José thrust out his enormous jaw. "We'll be right on your tail."

Joe rode back to the first fire, or rather to the spot where the first fire had been. Mort was stamping out the last coals. The other men were already on their horses and ready to move.

As the men strung out across the open range toward the Seven Up, Joe rode close to Mort. "Mort, there's somethin' queer back there."

"Frank?" asked Mort quickly.

"Yeah. He ain't showed up yet. What do you make of that?"

"Somebody ought to have tailed him," answered Mort.

"Somebody did. Lon thought it was a little too damned queer, too, and he rode after him to see what he was up to. You know, Mort, I never thought of Frank before. But Frank is just about Louie's size. And he's right next door to the L-Over-S."

"I don't think it's Frank Cross," said Mort slowly. "I'd sooner think it was some man on the

L-Over-S that knowed about Lem's affairs, that knowed about whatever was between Lem and Bess Quillan, if anything ever was. And—Coke Laughlin is a little guy that could pass for Lispy Louie, if you didn't see him too close and his face was covered."

Joe grunted and scowled at Mort helplessly. "The more you think about it the worse it gets. Shut up and ride."

CHAPTER XIV

REDEMPTION

A MAN can pursue a criminal course with seeming immunity only about so long. Then there comes a time when all men and all circumstances suddenly co-operate to conspire against him, and he is trapped. He is a phenomenally shrewd and clever man who can escape that combined set of opposing forces. That hour had come for Micky's captor. He had pursued his dark trail for years unhindered, but—he was both shrewd and clever, as well as desperate.

All night in the clearing among the trees he had kept that beacon fire burning, while Micky, helpless, dumb behind the brutal gag, drooped on the log in her bonds, and twice he had fallen asleep by the fire, and wakened and cursed himself: but Kurt Quillan had not come.

Kurt had gone to the north, a little to the west of the direction the Seven Up men had taken, and even in the moonlight seeking a fugitive in those gullies and forests became a wearing and futile thing. The Seven Up men turned south toward the ranch buildings, to get something to eat, coffee to drink, to rest a few hours and wait for daylight.

Only Kurt rode slowly on, because he visioned that thing which can be the gift of destiny, which may seem like the veriest chance, yet is in reality the reward granted a man whose vigilance and pertinacity are granted no lapse in the hours of crises. Somewhere in these hills rode Micky and her captor, the captor on his own horse, and Micky on the horse Kurt had been riding and which the captor had taken when he took Micky.

And if he, Kurt, rode on, weaving back and forth, watching and waiting, that reward of the vigilant might be granted him, dusk or dark, moonlight or dawn. He rode on.

And the man in the red chaps, furious at the failure of his attempt to trap Kurt, who was several miles to the east, decided to take his captive and move farther into the hills, as the first light of the breaking day began to seep like a fog through the trees. He released Micky from the log and ordered her onto the horse he had taken when Kurt had thrown himself from its back. The girl's muscles were so stiff she could scarcely keep her feet, they cramped with pain when she tried to move. Her throat ached and her mouth was dry and miserable from the gag. The man seized her arm and propelled her angrily ahead, when she was unable to move fast enough to satisfy him. His paramount idea now was to get well to the north before the Seven Up men could surround him.

And there he began to run afoul of those men and circumstances conspiring against him. They were gathering rapidly.

Bill Stagg had reached the Seven Up hours ago. Shortly after his arrival the Seven Up men came in, reporting that there was no sign of the man they sought, not to the east toward Lobo Pass. And Stagg said he was going to follow Kurt. He wanted to be in the hills by daylight. He mounted big white Skater and rode due north from the Seven Up buildings, west of the area the Seven Up men had combed.

Within three quarters of an hour after Stagg's departure, the Circle G men arrived, with little, fat Pete Gulick. With the Seven Up men, the entire crew of the Circle G save Benny Blaine rode north, a little east of the course Stagg had taken. In that hour, the Cross Bar men, all save Cross himself and the two cowboys who had gone with him toward the Crazy L, were cutting across the Circle G in a diagonal line, nearing the Seven Up south-west line. The L I men were close behind them.

The crew of the L-Over-S was moving north-east over the Cross Bar, nearing the Circle G south line. Forty-one men, the entire male population of the Seco range, converging to the spot where a killer skulked, a girl was held captive, and an outlaw fought desperately for redemption and a higher trail.

That the girl was almost a stranger, whom only a few of them had seen, and of whom most of them had only heard, mattered not at all. She was the doctor's niece, she had become one of them, and woman was not to be submitted to indignity on the Seco range.

The killer in the red chaps was mystery, and he was the first sinister and brutal figure the Seco had known. His continued existence was not to be suffered for another day. And Kurt was the boy they had known for most of his days, by sight or by hearsay, who had strangely turned to killing, himself, and confounded them all. Some of them would have shot him down, some of them would have seen him reprieved, all of them would be willing to listen if there was for him any reasonable defence. But not a man of them, able to get on a horse, could have been kept from the dénouement imminent there on the Seven Up.

And at the Seven Up ranch house, Doctor Mordan was sitting by Louie's bedside, and Louie was asking once again:

"Doc, am I goin' to die?"

This time there was a warming smile on Mordan's lean grey face, lifting the tired mouth under the white moustache. "No, Louie. You are not going to die. Not from this bullet wound. You will have to lie still for several days, before we'll dare move you. But I can say with confidence now that you aren't going to die. You came awfully close. You must have something to do in this world yet, Louie."

"Have they found Micky yet?"

"Not—yet, Louie."

"I've been athleep, haven't I?"

"You slept most of the night, Louie. Bill Stagg came, and the Circle G boys came, and you didn't know a thing about it. Mrs. Ryan is going to bring you a hot, nourishing breakfast."

"What do you thuppothe maybe I've got to do in thith world, doc?"

"I don't know, Louie. Perhaps you may know some little thing, that seems to you of no importance, but at the last minute may shove the last piece of the puzzle into place. The ways of the Almighty are strange."

"Ith it breaking daylight, doc?"

"Yes, Louie. It's been day for nearly an hour. I'll put up the blind. You'd better not talk any more right now. I'll go out and tell Mrs. Ryan you're awake and can have your breakfast."

He rose and went out of the room, and his

haggard grey eyes looked toward the front of the house, alive with swift hope, and his thin long body drew tensely erect, waiting, as he heard men ride into the yard. Then he went swiftly to swing wide the front door. But his tired shoulders drooped again. It was only the Cross Bar men, all save Cross and two of his boys, and part of the L I crew, who had overtaken them, along with Pete Gulick's man, Benny Blaine. There was no sign of Micky, or of Bill Stagg, or Kurt Quillan. Several of the men hailed the doctor, and he stepped out onto the porch.

"What's orders, doc? Pat here? Pete Gulick get here yet?"

"Pat and Pete are out with their men. I don't suppose there are any orders, Joe. You didn't see anything as you were working over this way?"

"Not a sign, doc."

"Well, I suspect you might as well go north and join in the hunt. There isn't anything else to do. And sitting around waiting isn't good for your sanity. I've been doing it all night."

A grim little silence fell, and the men turned awkwardly away, and the doctor went into the house and closed the door. He was whispering to himself.

"His ways aren't always my ways, and He never let me down yet. Whatever it is, whatever happens it will be all right. But I wish—I knew —where she is."

She was some eighteen miles north-west of the Seven Up, across the Seco Trail, bound onto the horse where her captor had placed her, half exhausted by physical suffering and fatigue. The horses were going slowly now. The man in the red chaps was prey to apprehension and worry. He was growing more desperate with every lengthening hour. He was getting farther into the hills, and going was becoming difficult. He had very often to take advantage of clear spots, which were dangerously exposing, if he would advance at all, and advance he must.

He rode with his hand on the edge of his thigh near his gun, his harried eyes sharply surveying every yard of terrain as he proceeded. He wished he were free of the girl now, but he had told the truth when he had said he feared the reprisal killing her would precipitate. Better leave her back here somewhere for someone to find later. But he still hoped that his possession of her would draw Quillan into his line of fire.

For some time now Quillan had been veering more directly west. The man in the red chaps had been forced toward the east, by the sheer lie of the land and the natural obstructions he encountered as he worked deeper into the hills. The man's ears were strained to the sharpness a fugitive's ears know.

He heard the sound of a horse's feet on rock. He looked frantically about for cover. There was none for several yards in any direction, save to the east.

This was one of those dangerous open spots, of which he must take advantage if he would advance to the north at all. The man in the red chaps listened again intently. One horse. Only one. Then he gave a harsh, leering laugh, pulled his mount to a halt, and leaped from the saddle.

The advancing horse, almost in sight now beyond a fringe of brush to the east, was a Seven Up horse. Kurt Quillan was on its back. Kurt had no warning. He was riding slowly, his cold blue eyes clear wells in which despair had kindled its consuming flame. He rode out of the brush into the clear, and even the horse he rode must have felt then the might of the driving force that leaped and quivered about him. The horse stopped.

There is a belief that when a man faces death, all his past life crowds before his eyes. That was not true of Kurt Quillan. He knew that death was there, and would strike at him within another instant; but all of the past that rose to confront him was the section of it which had endured since the hour when he first looked up from the bed, where he lay with a broken jaw, and gazed into Micky's face.

He could not see much of her face now, in that unreal vision that seemed almost to swim, as if his eyes were blurred with moisture, or as if he were struck in the stomach by nausea. The two horses stood there, in the clear space before him, broadside toward him. The first horse was riderless. On the second horse Micky Blue sat tied into the saddle. A handkerchief was bound tightly about her face. Her pale blonde hair was a dishevelled, curling mass, dusted with silver by the sun. Her face was without colour. Her amber eyes were wide upon him, in a kind of numb horror that was hushed by resignation, and a pride in him, for all he could have given her, for all he might have been, had it been granted him to survive. There was no shrinking, no weakness of hysteria.

This was the girl who had said there was no percentage in making a fool of yourself. It was also the girl who had said: "There is another world waiting, and I'll meet you there some day."

He knew then that she was right. If this paid the score, it was still worth it. And surely, this must pay the score—because he had no chance; this must be some inescapable reprisal ordered by a higher power.

His enemy, the small man in the red chaps, stood behind Micky's horse, his body completely hidden by the horse, nothing of him showing but the rim of his tan, stained hat thrusting out from behind the girl's back, the ragged ends of his chaps below the horse's belly, and the bore of his gun across the horse's back pointing straight at Kurt's breast.

As Kurt pulled his feet free of his stirrups, the gun across the horse's back, in the hand of the man in the red chaps, belched and crashed. The bullet hit Kurt high in the right shoulder. Micky's horse quivered and started.

With a supreme effort, Quillan flung himself from his own mount, and as he struck the ground both guns were out. The facility and ease with which he levelled them, lying there on his stomach, was so great that both the speed and accuracy with which it was done would have been lost to a beholder. It was lost to Micky's unwinking, exalted gaze.

Kurt's right-hand gun blasted its defiant answer. The bullet passed between the horse's hind legs and shattered the bone in the small man's right shin. It brought him to his knees. Kurt's left-hand gun spoke. That bullet tore into the small man's groin.

And now the man in the red chaps was shooting again, and the horse beneath Micky quivered and started, and leaped ahead, and stopped, leaving the two men facing each other on the ground.

The small man's next shot struck Kurt in the chest. He felt it plough in. He said aloud:

"If this is to be my last, I might as well make a good job of it."

And the two guns in his hands crashed together, again, and again. And they were empty. The small man in the red chaps lay still. His gun had fallen to the ground. It was empty also. Kurt's brain, as clear as if bathed in some white, revealing light, functioned in one straight line. He had felt every bullet strike. His wide eyes, the cleanest, coldest blue they had ever been, strove to see Micky's face.

He spoke clearly just one word:

"Eight."

And collapsed flat upon his face. But just before he fell so, he smiled. The two dimples drove deep into the faintly coloured cheeks. Then he lay still, and the sun built its fire in his chestnut hair.

Micky raised her gaze. Which way did man's spirit go, up, or out, or merely away? She turned slowly in the saddle and looked back at the man in the red chaps. He was a mangled, bloody mass. He, too, had paid his score, in full. She was conscious of a queer exaltation. She bowed her head, and a lightness seized her. She fainted.

She still huddled there, quite unconscious, fifteen minutes later, when big white Skater came racing into the clearing. Stagg brought the gelding to such a wild halt that the horse stumbled for footing. Behind Stagg rode Pete Gulick. Stagg turned his gaze upon Gulick, beyond all words. Then he raised his gun and fired three times into the air, and got down from the saddle, slowly, wearily, as if all will to locomotion had been drained from him.

Gulick dismounted, and stood still. His round fat face was a stiff mask of sorrow.

"Could you do it?" he asked, and wet his lips, and swallowed. "Just to be sure?" He made a small gesture toward Micky's inert body. "Before she comes to, yet?"

Stagg made no answer, save to walk toward the body that lay nearest, the lithe long figure of Kurt. He stood over it for a moment as if this were something he could not quite do. Then he bent, laid one hand gently on Kurt's shoulder, and turned the body over. There was one bullet hole and a round patch of crimson high in the right shoulder. There were two bullet holes in the chest, one squarely over the heart. The entire shirt front was a mass of blood. He had fallen with his left arm doubled under him, against his chest, and the sleeve was saturated with blood. There was no bullet hole in the sleeve.

"So it had to be this way!" The voice was Micky's. Stagg and Gulick both turned their heads toward her. The blast of Stagg's signal had dragged her back to consciousness. She sat erect, with that still exalted air of pride clothing her like a radiant garment.

"Yes," said Stagg. "He is quite—dead."

He walked on to the body of the man in the red chaps, and bent a little, and blinked, and his black eyes stared. "My gad," he said slowly, "he took all twelve bullets! Kurt emptied both guns into him."

253

"Yah." Gulick's voice quavered. "But, Himmel! Who is he? Pull dot rag off mit his face!"

From east and west, men called by that significant signal of Stagg's, heralded their approach in thundering horses' hoofs, as Stagg leaned to draw aside from the small man's face the blood-wet bandanna, twice as red as it had ever been before.

And Gulick stared, and again wet his lips, and half whispered. "Himmel! Nein! It couldn't be!"

In the ranch house at the Seven Up, like an echo, Doctor Mordan was saying the same words. "Heavens, no! It couldn't be."

The remaining men of the Seco, who had been approaching the Seven Up, all save Frank Cross, were gathered in the room where Louie lay, and Louie had just said stubbornly:

"It'th Lon Ivey! It hath to be Lon Ivey." And when the doctor replied that it couldn't be, Louie's one good eye fixed on the doctor's face. "Thomehow I jutht know it. Lithten—thomebody ith comin'."

Mrs. Ryan, pale with weariness, but upheld by unprecedented excitement, hurried out to open the front door as the sound of a buckboard approaching and stopping before the house reached all their ears.

She swung back the door, and there, coming across the porch toward her, was Martha Strickland, Martha Laughlin now, and Coke

Laughlin was close behind her. Martha reached out both her hands.

"Oh, Nanny, my dear! This is a terrible thing! Coke and I came back as soon as we got Rocky's telegram. And when Pete Gulick's man told us what was happening, we hitched up the buckboard and started immediately, but we had to come by the Cross Bar road, and it took us longer than the boys. Nanny, Nanny! I must see the doctor. I know the truth. I know what must be all of the truth."

"Steady, honey!" Laughlin's arm went around her, and his dark, handsome face was set with concern. "Don't go to pieces."

"Oh, come in! Come in!" cried Mrs. Ryan in relief. "We're all of us about crazy with worry. If you can tell us anything to help! Right this way, Martha. The doctor is in Pat's room, with Louie and some of the men." She bustled ahead, and the Laughlins followed in a tense and nervous eagerness.

Mordan turned quickly to see who had come, and his face lighted with a surprise that smoothed, a little, some of the lines on his weary grey visage. "Why, Mrs. Strick—Mrs. Laughlin!"

Martha Laughlin went straight to him. "Doctor, we had to come. There's some awful mistake, and I know I can help to set it right. There can be no deed leaving Kurt the L-Over-S. Lem owned it long before Bess Quillan came. He never would

255

have sold it to any one. I know. Lem often told me all about it.

"I had hoped so long that he could bring things right for Kurt, and then he was—killed. And I was afraid it was forever too late. He never could do anything with Ivey. Because Ivey held that—that terrible happening over him. And Lem had hoped to the last that Kurt would never have to know."

The doctor interrupted. "Sit down, Mrs. Laughlin. Mrs. Ryan, bring me a glass of water. Keep still for a moment, Mrs. Laughlin. Please." He gently forced her into the chair by Louie's bedside. From his kit he took a little long bottle, and out of the bottle a white paper folded over white powder. He closed the kit as Mrs. Ryan hurried into the room, accepted the glass from her hand, and shook the powder into it. "Drink this, Mrs. Laughlin, and sit still. You're going to break, yourself, if you don't take this business a little easier. Drink it down. That's the girl!"

He set the emptied glass on the near little square table, and forced a casual smile. "Now you listen, while I talk a minute, and get your breath. I'll tell you what Bill Stagg learned from Lon, and you can fill in the lapses."

And he recounted concisely the story Ivey had related to Stagg, concerning that tragic night in the pass when Bess had come to her death, and the subsequent events. "Now, if you know any-

256

thing more than that, tell us. But don't let yourself get so wrought up again. And remember that no one wants to make you any trouble, but that wedding certificate exists, and the deed to the L-Over-S, and Stagg saw them, and says they are absolutely legal."

"Yeth, and I thaw 'em!" said Louie, his one good eye fixed earnestly on Mrs. Laughlin's face. "I've got 'em."

"But Lem never sold the L-Over-S," Martha Laughlin protested. "There's some crooked work somewhere, doctor! Lon told Bill Stagg the truth, most of the truth, but he mixed the truth so smoothly with lies! And he took Bill in, he fooled him, just as he fooled Bess Quillan. He did meet her in Madder Junction, but he was not there with any herd. He had no herd! He was just a scheming drifter. He had nothing. He made her believe he had a ranch, when he was only a hand on the L I. Not a very good hand, either. Bess always believed he got a glimpse of the money she slipped into her carpet bag there in the station, and made his plans right then.

"He told her Lem had left this country, he offered her a place as housekeeper on his ranch. She had no place to turn, and he was so smooth. She went to the L I with him, only, of course, it wasn't the L I then. Bess never wrote any letter to explain to Lem. She never knew Lem was here till after she'd married Ivey. That was when she left him, when she heard that, and faced him with it, and he went into a fury, and she was afraid of him."

"But how do you know all this, Mrs. Laughlin?" Mordan asked.

"Why, Bess told Lem herself! When she left Lon, she inquired the way to the L-Over-S, at Seco Springs, and came straight to Lem. She told him what had happened to her, and it broke him all up. He hadn't known what had become of her. He never stopped loving her. She told him she was leaving Ivey, and she was getting a divorce from him, and after it was all over, she would come back and marry Lem. But she was afraid of Ivey. She was afraid he'd follow her, and she wanted Lem to ride with her to the pass, to see her safe out of the country.

"And that—that's another place Lon lied to Bill Stagg. Lon did not ride with Bess to the pass; he followed her and Lem. She had her wedding certificate and some other paper in the bosom of her dress, she told Lem so, but she didn't say what the other paper was. Lem told me she didn't. Lem rode with her almost to the pass, over the Circle G road, and by then she felt certain she was safe, and urged him to turn back. It was only such a short way through the pass and on to Madder Junction. They hadn't seen any sign of Ivey anywhere, and Lem didn't believe Ivey could be very vicious anyway, so he did turn back.

"But Lon had followed by Seco Trail, and when he saw Lem turn back, he rode up and cornered Bess, and attacked her, fighting for those papers in her dress. Bess fought back, screaming, and he dragged her off her horse, and knocked Kurt to the ground. She screamed as loud as she could, hoping Lem would hear. Lem hadn't gone far, he had stopped and turned around and started to overtake her; he was worried about her, and he had decided to insist on going to Madder Junction with her. He came into sight of her at her first scream. He saw the whole thing.

"When Lem came racing up, Lon snatched something from Bess's dress, and knocked her down, and jumped onto his horse. Lem started firing at him, and Lon started firing back, and Bess staggered to her feet and got between them. Lem didn't mean to kill her. It was an accident. It ruined his whole life. He never got over it. When he saw her fall, he knew by the way she was shot that she'd been killed instantly. His horse had blundered back into the brush, frightened. Lem went after the horse so he could pursue Lon. While he was catching the horse, another rider came dashing out of the pass and rode after Lon. Lem heard them both firing as they disappeared in the dusk. He never knew the other man was Bill Stagg.

"And he went back to Bess, and picked Kurt up. That's the truth of the thing, doctor. He loved

Kurt like his own son. It broke his heart when Kurt grew up and started killing people. He and Lon were always at outs. He was always trying to get those papers back, and Lon held it over him that if he ever made a move he would reveal the fact that Lem had killed Bess, and Lem didn't want Kurt to know."

"And the other paper," said the doctor gently, "was the deed to the L-Over-S."

"Oh, dear Lord, it couldn't be!" Martha Laughlin's lips quivered. "Lem would have told me! He loved Kurt so much. He never even blamed Kurt for killing him, Stagg said. He thought Kurt had been impelled by some awful mistake—or that maybe Lon had at last told Kurt—about Bess. So he knew the truth as he died. If we'd only known what made Kurt go bad—he'd been such a fine boy—"

"He'th thtill thwell," said Lispy Louie. "He never drew on a man firtht in hith life. That'th why I wathn't afraid to go up to him. That'th why he wouldn't thhoot me, even when he thought I jumped him. Jutht like all thothe other fellath jumped him. I know. I picked up one of 'em Kurt had thhot, and he wath dyin', and he told me it wath hith own fault, he'd jumped Kurt firtht. And thomehow I've always believed it wath the thame with the otherth. I know the man in the red chapth wath Lon Ivey. I've been knowin' it better every hour thinthe I been layin' here."

260

"It would be like Ivey," said Martha Laughlin. "But I don't see—there he was on his own ranch when the man in the red chaps shot you and Kurt. He was here on the Seven Up when you saw the man kill Barnes."

"Wait!" Louie's voice rose almost to a shout. "I know! I know. I wath thure I'd get it if I figgered long enough. Joe—did you thee Lon at the camp fire, or at the houthe when you thtarted? Did you thee him with your own eyeth?"

"Why, no." Joe shook his head. "But I heard him. I yelled and he answered. And José said he was there."

Louie was quivering with excitement. "Did Pat thee him, Mithuth Ryan?"

"N-n-no, Louie. But José said he was waiting down the road a piece, so Pat told me."

"Don't you get it?" cried Louie, his greasy face sweating in excitement, his cocked eye rolling wildly. "You didn't thee him—you heard him—Jothay thaid he wath there! Jothay wath in with him! Jothay could mock him till you'd thwear it wath Lon only ten feet away. I've heard him. He didn't come over here with the herd! He rode a wayth with 'em and turned back, to kill Barnth, who he had tied up thomewhere. And Jothay covered it. Lon knew Bill wath comin'. He wath jutht waitin' out there in the night for Bill to thhow up, and he told Bill all that about Beth, mixin' it with lieth, to throw Bill off the track.

261

"And he wathn't back there with the pothee. Jothay covered that, too. He wath followin' Kurt and me, and he jumped uth the firtht chanthe he got. And he thtole Micky to draw Kurt on and—"

"Louie!" Mordan laid a hand over the excited little man's mouth. "This won't do. Keep still. You've said plenty. I told you you had something to live for. I know now why Micky wanted Bill to ask Kurt why he hadn't shot at you. She read the man better than any of us. Mrs. Ryan! Horsemen! Maybe it's some word—" The doctor's voice trailed away from the words he could not say.

But Mrs. Ryan had no need to go to the front door. It opened, and a man's footsteps hurried through the front room, down the hall, and the waiting gaze of the group turned to the doorway of the bedroom.

Frank Cross stepped into sight. "Anybody get Ivey?"

Mordan shook his head helplessly. "Not that I know. Was it Ivey, Frank?"

"Yes. I'd suspected it for days. That's why I took two of the boys and started for the L I. I asked for Ivey all along the line, and all along the line they sent me north, till I reached José Sanchez. He said the boss was right around there somewhere. I went on looking, and I heard a horse passing in the brush. I called. Ivey answered. And I knew Ivey wasn't there. I knew it was José answering. It took me nearly an hour to corner him, but I did it! So that finally I looked through the brush and saw him do it, heard Ivey's voice, coming out of that mouth above José's monstrous jaw. I knew then. I stepped out and let him have it, right between the eyes. I came on here, working over the north of the open range and the Circle G. But I didn't find any trace of Ivey. I—"

Cross interrupted himself and turned as heavy steps ran up the front-porch stairs, the door burst open, and little fat Pete Gulick came rushing in, and Cross backed into the bedroom, and eyes and breath held at the sight of Gulick's countenance. It looked almost thin, dried and yellowed with an unbearable grief.

"Stagg—he sent me to tell you, yet." Even his voice was dry and thinned with grief. "Der boys iss all coming. Micky is all right. Kurt, he got her, doc. We heard der shots und come on der run. Kurt—he emptied both guns into Ivey. Und—und he took four of Ivey's bullets. Der boys is bringing dem. Dey is both—both dead. I—I—oh, Himmel, doc! Let me sit down or I don't stand somethings more."

Mrs. Laughlin began to sob softly. "Oh, my poor Kurt. I loved him, too, doctor."

"It ain't right! It ain't fair!" Little Louie's eyes were wet, the cocked and the good one. "He thaid he wanted to thit in on a new game. There ain't no—"

"Hush!" said Mordan. His thin long frame drooped, but his lined grey face was stilled into calm. "Whatever He decrees is right. If that was the way Kurt had to pay, it must have been best. Hush. Here they come."

Fraught silence fell over the room, the kind of silence that falls where sleep those who may never waken again till the last trumpet calls. The sound of many horses ridden slowly came to a stop outside. Footfalls, light, yet slow, ascended the steps into the house, and Stagg appeared in the doorway, all the other men crowding behind him, Kurt's limp body cradled in his arms, Kurt's lolling chestnut head burning its fire against his shoulder. Beside Stagg walked Micky, her head high, that same exalted pride clothing her like a garment.

Stagg stood still, and Mordan's eyes leaped to the great stain of blood on Kurt's breast. The doctor motioned silently to the bed, and again Stagg moved lightly but slowly forward, and laid Kurt's body beside little Louie. The doctor's gaze passed over the bullet holes in the breast of the shirt. He tried to speak, failed, and tried again.

"No man on earth—could have done anything —for him. He—Micky! My dear—" His arms went around his niece.

Her amber eyes shone with that white pride. "He accepted his way. He tallied his score. He washed it clean as a crystal."

"Yes. He—he—" The doctor's gaze widened, stared, fixed on Kurt. He almost shoved his niece from him. He bent over the bed. "Bill! Did you say this man is dead!"

"I thought he was dead till I picked him up." Stagg's black eyes were wells of weariness and pain. "I saw then that he was barely breathing. I didn't say anything. I knew, as you just said, that no man could do anything for him. And—for Micky—I saw no use in rousing a hope that had to be in vain. I wish you hadn't said it—till we'd got her away."

"While there's life there's hope!" said Mordan harshly. "Stand back while I look at this boy!"

He leaned over Kurt, and his deft hands flashed into motion. Little Louie's cocked eye was still, staring into space, his one good eye on Mordan's tense grey countenance.

Stagg's gaze went to Micky, oblivious to the packed gathering of those hushed men of the Seco range, to Micky, whom he had striven to save from this. She had seen Kurt die once. Bitter draught, that she must see him die again. She was like something that feared to live, yet clung to life because it must. Her delicate face, he thought, was what an angel's face must be, when it lifted to its Lord. Her amber eyes were unearthly lights. He remembered that he had read somewhere that there was an angel, a kind of mythical angel, that embodied a beautiful thought. That angel must look as Micky looked now. Only he couldn't remember the angel's name. What was it? It began with an S. Why, yes, that was it! Memory leaped; of course, that was it.

He said aloud, "Yes, of course—San—Sandalphon!"

Micky didn't hear him.

Louie whispered: "Than—than what?"

Stagg's organ tones resounded softly. "Sandalphon." His eyes were still on Micky's face. "Sandalphon, the angel of prayer. He takes the prayers of men, and weaves them into crowns, to present to his God. He's the mortal's go-between, old-timer. Sandalphon—angel of—prayer."

Doctor Mordan raised to his long thin height. His grey face was alight, as if he had encountered something that was beyond the reach and understanding of any one related to earth, least of all his humble and striving self. His voice was muted, yet it seemed to shimmer, as glass dust shimmers in a beam of sun. He said:

"He has never let me down!"

"Who?" said little Louie.

The doctor's smile erased half the lines on his face. He addressed the transfixed crowd in the room. "Men—have you any verdict?"

Rocky Andover answered. "We didn't understand. We didn't know what he was. We didn't know what had been done to him. I guess any of

266

us would give all we've got to bring him back and tell him so."

Mordan's face flushed with even brighter light. "He hasn't gone very far, Rocky. In all my experience, I have never seen anything like this. One bullet, it must have slanted up from below him, when he sat on his horse, perhaps, simply cut through the flesh between the clavicle and the scapula. It never even touched bone. It simply bored through skin and a little flesh."

"Doctor—" Stagg groped. "You're technical."

"I'm sorry. It went between the collar bone and the shoulder blade. The two holes in the shirt front—one bullet hit something and caromed; he must have been lying on his stomach from then on; the bullet struck into the flesh of his left breast, it had barely enough force left to lodge there, loose, it's lying upon the sternum—the breast bone. One simply raked down his skin along the stomach and lodged against his gun belt, merely burned the skin. The worst one slid under the cuff of his left sleeve and ploughed through the flesh of his lower arm from above the wrist to the elbow. It's loose in his sleeve. It didn't even cut an artery.

"When he fell on the arm, the pressure of his body gradually stopped the bleeding. That's where all the blood on his chest came from; from his arm. For a man who has tried to stop eight bullets he'd done a damned poor job of it.

There's practically nothing the matter with him."

"Uncle Dan!"

"Yes, my dear. I told you there was such a thing as—destiny."

"But"—Stagg's organ tones groped again—"he's so still, he's hardly breathing—"

"He's asleep!" Mordan almost snorted. "That's the light breathing of exhaustion, man! Have you stopped to think how long it's been since that boy has had any sleep? He left my house night before last; he's been riding, fighting, eating when he could, and had no sleep since then. A little bullet shock knocked him out, and he simply went to sleep. I am not going to waken him if I can help it. The sleep will do him more good than anything else. All he needs is nourishment, a little cleaning up, and a good bit of rest."

"Doctor." Martha Laughlin rose from the chair beside the bed. "Before he wakes, this one last thing. I must see that deed, somehow. He has been my son, too. If Bess really purchased the L-Over-S, it is his. Coke and I—we—maybe he would let us stay on, doctor. I know he would. Where can I see the deed?"

"Here," answered Bill Stagg. "Excuse me, Louie, but I got it, after you went out yesterday morning, and brought it along." He drew the paper from his pocket and extended it toward Mrs. Laughlin. "I thought we might need it for something."

Martha Laughlin took it with reluctant and yet eager fingers. She unfolded it, and her eyes lighted with sudden understanding. "Why, this isn't a deed to the L-Over-S Ranch. It's a deed to the L I. These east boundary markers absolutely prove it!" Something halfway between a sob and an hysterical laugh shook her voice. "Don't you see the way the letters are all run together? Lovers, not L-Over-S! Lovers! When Bess first came, when Lon was merely working there, Jack Lovers owned it. It was known then simply as the Lovers ranch."

"By Jiminy!" cried fat little Pete Gulick. "I remember dot! I vas knowing Jack Lovers mine-self! But he just vent avay, already, und der ranch vas der L I, und I never t'ought noddings about it."

Bill Stagg straightened to his astounding height. His deep voice rolled through the room. "There is a bigger justice than men can deal. Bess's dreams were in that house. In that ranch. She wanted it for her son."

"Yes." Mordan's voice cut in, sharp and commanding. "And for that son's sake, all of you move out of here. I have to do a few things for him. They're little enough, but they're important. And I don't want him wakened by all your racket. Come along. Get out into the other part of the house, please."

They went. In a silent file, ready to burst into

269

excited conversation once they were beyond the room where Kurt Quillan lay in reviving sleep. Stagg was one of the last to go, and Louie's abashed voice halted him.

"Bill! You know—you and me, on the Crazy L—right next door—we could have thome thwell timeth, maybe."

Stagg smiled down at him. "I'll be there, Louie! Try to keep me away!"

"Please go, Bill!" said Mordan anxiously. "I want to get those wounds cleaned and dressed."

Stagg went quietly out and closed the door behind him. Only Micky remained, facing the doctor with that hot high pride.

"Should I go, too, Uncle Dan?"

"No, sweet." The voice came from the bed.

Both Micky and the doctor turned. From beside little Louie, Kurt raised his eyes; clear eyes, cool clean blue. The force that was Kurt Quillan was pent no longer. It spread and flowered. Unharried, potent and serene, it quivered in the air about him like a light. He smiled. The dimples at the corners of his full curved mouth drove deep. The sun from the window burned in his chestnut hair.

"No, sweet," he repeated, and the tone sang like the muted A string of a guitar. "You do not go from me—ever."

Center Point Publishing
600 Brooks Road ● PO Box 1
Thorndike ME 04986-0001 USA

(207) 568-3717

US & Canada:
1 800 929-9108
www.centerpointlargeprint.com